OPERATOR 5:
SIEGE OF THE THOUSAND PATRIOTS

SECRET SERVICE OPERATOR #5™

AMERICA'S UNDERCOVER ACE

SIEGE OF THE THOUSAND PATRIOTS

By Curtis Steele

POPULAR PUBLICATIONS • 2021

PUBLISHING HISTORY

"Siege of the Thousand Patriots" originally appeared in the February, 1937 (Vol. 8, No. 3) issue of *Operator #5* magazine. Copyright © 2021 by Argosy Communications, Inc. All rights reserved.

CHAPTER 1
DOWN THE PACIFIC SLOPE

A GENTLE breeze from the Hudson tugged at the purple flag of the Central Empire, flying in sinister triumph from the steeple of St. Patrick's Cathedral in New York City. That flag, with its gruesome emblem of the crossed broadswords and the severed head, was now flying over every city in the United States from the eastern seaboard to the Rocky Mountains. Under that standard, the goose-stepping cohorts of Rudolph I, ruler of the Central Empire, master of Europe and Asia, had pushed the American Defense Forces back to the last natural barrier afforded by the topography of the United States.

And now the news had arrived that the Imperial Armies under Marshal Kremer had crossed the Rockies at a dozen points and were pushing inexorably toward the Pacific.

To celebrate this news, Rudolph I had ordained for the following Sunday, in St. Patrick's Cathedral, the solemn ceremony of his coronation as Emperor of America. The crowning glory of Rudolph's cruel career was to be also the occasion for the greatest degradation of the citizens of America; for the official coronation of Rudolph I, would convert those millions of Americans who had survived the Purple Invasion from free citizens of a free country into virtual serfdom under as autocratic an imperial government as had ever ruled upon the face of the earth.

Seven months before, the Purple Empire had launched its

great offensive against America. Equipped with an army which had become the most powerful fighting machine in the world, the Emperor of the Central Empire had carried fire and sword and destruction across the country. America had not been prepared to meet adequately the threat of this highly milita-

A long yell rose from the ranks of the
Canadian Lancers, and the long wicked guns
at the top of the slope thundered reply.

rized power. For years our propagandists of peace and disarma-
ment had crippled our own plans for defensive preparedness.
Our biggest guns were no longer a match for the huge guns

of the Central Empire; our air force could not make bravery and courage take the place of numbers and equipment. We had relied too much on the Atlantic and the Pacific Oceans as natural defenses. The Purple Empire had overcome the defense of the Atlantic Ocean by launching a fleet gathered from every quarter of the globe.

Stubbornly, our defense forces had yielded ground foot by foot and inch by inch. Patriots sacrificed their lives in vain. Slowly we were driven back. And now, on the three hundred and first day of the Purple Invasion, an alien Emperor was at last to impose his rule upon America.

In the streets around St. Patrick's Cathedral the hum of activity gave evidence of the preparations that were being made for Rudolph's coronation. Hundreds of Americans, working under forced labor, were toiling to erect a huge grandstand where the nobility of the Central Empire would sit for the ceremony. Other hundreds of civilian prisoners were hard at work upon a huge triumphal arch which spanned Fifth Avenue just below the cathedral.

The arch rose two hundred feet into the air, and upon its granite blocks were depicted the scenes of victories of the Purple Empire over the American Defense Forces. Upon the center block, which formed the keystone of the arch, there had been sculptured the brutal device of the Central Empire—the insignia of the severed head and the crossed broadswords.

The Americans who labored upon this monument to their disgrace did so with bitterness in their hearts, goaded on by the keen bayonets of Central Empire troopers. These Americans would have been very glad to throw down their tools and invite death by refusing to perform any further work; but they dared not do so, for Baron Julian Flexner, the Emperor's Prime Minister, had selected them carefully, making sure that each of the civilians chosen for this task had a wife and children. Those wives and those children would die miserably if these men rebelled. And so they toiled, expending the sweat of their bodies for the greater glory of their conqueror.

BUT THE bitterness in the hearts of these men might have been somewhat alleviated had they seen the two persons who stood on Fifth Avenue not far away from them, watching the toilers.

These two persons were careful to act in such a manner as not to attract the attention of the Central Empire patrols which were constantly passing. They were dressed in the ordinary civilian clothes of American residents of the occupied territory.

The younger of the two was slender, with smooth features and sparkling blue eyes. He must have been very young indeed, for there was not a trace of beard upon his smooth face. The other was a tall, powerfully-built, square-jawed man with the face and shoulders of a fighter.

Each wore a white button in the overcoat lapel. These white buttons carried the insignia of the severed head and the crossed broadswords, together with a number. The younger one's number was A-1209, the older one's B-1600. These buttons were distributed to all civilians by the governor of the conquered territory. They signified that the civilians wearing them had complied with all the requirements of the Central Empire Army of Occupation, and were permitted to be abroad in the streets during the daylight hours from eight in the morning to five in the evening. Any civilian found in the street without such a button was summarily executed without even an opportunity to explain his presence.

Now, the passing patrols cast casual glances at the buttons, and went on, leaving the two unmolested. They stood there, glancing about expectantly, as if they were awaiting someone. Abruptly, the shorter of the two, Number A-1209, nudged his companion. "Here comes Lacord, Mac. Make it fast, now. We mustn't attract too much attention."

The man addressed as Mac nodded. He glanced up the street toward where a short, stocky man was strolling, apparently aimlessly, down Fifth Avenue. This was Hiram Lacord, former Mayor of New York. He, too, wore a white button in his lapel. When the troops of the Purple Emperor had occupied New York, Lacord had been captured and forced to swear the oath of allegiance to the Emperor, together with thousands of other Americans. But he had never ceased to hope and plan for the day when America might once more rid itself of the tyranny of this ruthless oppressor.

He threw a keen glance at the two civilians, and noted the green-and-blue striped neckties which they both wore, which were identical to the one he himself was wearing. He gave no sign of recognition, except for a quick glance which he threw around to note whether they were observed. Then he angled over so as to pass close to them.

When he had come abreast of the two, Number B-1600 took

a cigarette from his pocket, and called out to him: "Say, brother, have you got a match?"

Lacord stopped, fished in his pocket, and produced a book of matches which he handed over slowly. At the same time he said: "A match is a small thing, my friend."

Number B-1600 was lighting his cigarette. He replied between puffs: "A small match may start a great conflagration."

Lacord's face was expressionless. But there was a quick eagerness in his voice. "You'll be MacTavish, then. What is your message?"

MacTavish spoke quickly, as he handed back the matches. "We plan to stop the coronation. We need a hundred good men, patriots who are not afraid to die. Can you get that many men together by tonight?"

"Yes, that I can. But where? The Purple troops are all over the city. We tried to hold secret meetings before, but they've raided us—"

"I don't think they'll raid us this time," MacTavish told him grimly. "We'll meet in the ruins of the old Polo Grounds at the approach to the Macombs Dam Bridge. My friend and I looked the place over this morning. It was badly smashed up when the Purple Navy bombarded New York, and I notice the patrols are pretty thin up there."

Lacord nodded in agreement. "That's a good place. I'll have the men there tonight. Depend on me." He looked at MacTavish's companion. "Is he all right?" he asked doubtfully. "He looks rather young—"

MacTavish grinned. "You don't have to worry on that score,

Lacord. This isn't a 'he'; it's a 'she.' Permit me to introduce Miss Nan Christopher—the sister of Operator 5!"

Lacord's face suddenly paled. He whistled under his breath. "You shouldn't have come, Miss Christopher. It's dangerous. There's a reward on your head, as well as on that of your brother. If Rudolph ever got his hands on you—God, I wouldn't envy you!"

Nan Christopher smiled tightly. "I'll try to see to it, Mr. Lacord, that Rudolph doesn't get his hands on me."

Lacord was studying her closely. "I think you'll get by all right, Miss Christopher." There was admiration in his glance. "You're a wonderful actress. You carry yourself just like a young man. I'd never suspect you to be a woman. But you must be careful just the same. Now that MacTavish has told me who you are, I can see the resemblance to your brother. You're his twin sister, and you look exactly like him. You don't know how many men Rudolph and Baron Flexner have out, hunting for Operator 5. They're likely to notice the resemblance too—"

"I've got to take that chance," Nan Christopher said hurriedly. "And we'd better not be seen talking together any more. That Central Empire lieutenant across the street has been looking at us suspiciously."

"I'll go, then," Lacord said. "But first tell me—how goes it at the Rockies?"

"Poorly," MacTavish said with a sudden somberness in his voice. "They've pushed our line back across the Continental Divide. We can't match their big guns. Soon they'll drive us into the Pacific. If we can manage to stop this coronation by some

8

brilliant *coup*, it will bolster the morale of the American Defense Force. That's why Operator 5 allowed us to come here and try."

Nan Christopher suddenly said urgently: "Go quickly, Mr. Lacord. That lieutenant is coming over here to question us. Don't stop or look back. Go at once and round up the men for tonight's meeting—and don't worry about us. We won't be detained."

Lacord appeared genuinely worried, but he did as Nan told him. He walked Up Fifth Avenue toward St. Patrick's Cathedral, without looking back.

MacTAVISH AND Nan Christopher started in the other direction, walking casually, trying to seem as if they had not noticed the Central Empire lieutenant who was crossing the street in their direction.

The lieutenant's eyes were narrowed suspiciously, and he seemed to be on the point of calling out and ordering Lacord to stop. He watched MacTavish and Nan go in one direction, and Lacord in the other, all three apparently strolling innocently through the streets. He had seen the white buttons on the lapels of all of them, and he knew this meant that they had passed the inspection of the authorities, and had complied with the forced labor requirements. What he did not know was that MacTavish and Nan Christopher had obtained their buttons from two American civilians whom they had met upon arriving in New York.

His gaze lingered upon them for a moment, then he shrugged and was about to turn back, when he suddenly frowned. His eyes had caught sight of a suspicious bulge in MacTavish's back pocket, under the overcoat. That bulge suggested a revolver.

The lieutenant's eyes narrowed. Now he hesitated no longer. He started off after the two, hurrying briskly, and caught up with them at the corner just as they were about to turn into the side street.

He tapped MacTavish on the shoulder, said arrogantly: "Stop! You will both give an account of yourselves."

MacTavish froze, and turned slowly, his lips tightening into a thin, grim line. His hand began to work at the buttons of his overcoat so that he could swing it back to get at the gun in his hip pocket.

Nan Christopher kicked him in the shins warningly, at the same time that she said genially to the Central Empire officer: "With pleasure, Lieutenant. Here are my credentials."

From her coat pocket she extracted the *dossier* which every civilian was required to carry about with him. It was a sheet of paper, six inches long and three inches wide. At the top was engraved the crossed broadswords and the severed head of the Central Empire. Underneath, appeared the words:

RUDOLPH I, REX IMPERATOR

Underneath appeared the information that the bearer was Frank Stanford, age eighteen, an actor by profession. It bore the seal and the stamp of the Commandant of the Occupied Territory of New York, Baron von Grunau. At the bottom of the sheet were two rows of numbered squares, thirty in all, each bearing a number representing a day of the month. Since each civilian in the occupied territory was required to perform four hours of labor each day for the Central Empire, it was necessary to carry this *dossier* always. Each day that the required labor was performed, the corresponding square was stamped officially by the overseer in charge of the labor squad. Frank Stanford's squares were duly stamped up to date.

The lieutenant examined the *dossier* very closely, and grunted as he noticed that everything was in order. He folded it up, but did not return it to Nan. Instead he extended his hand to

NAN

MacTavish. "Let me have your *dossier!*" he demanded curtly. MacTavish opened his coat, produced the paper from the inside pocket. It showed that he was John Stanford, age forty-six, also an actor. His labor squares were also duly stamped. The lieutenant glanced up at him suspiciously, then looked at Nan, and frowned. He appraised them both carefully, then said to MacTavish: "You are this young man's father?"

MacTavish nodded. "We're both, actors, Lieutenant—and I guess we're pretty good ones, at that."

Nan Christopher put an arm around MacTavish's waist, glanced up at him affectionately, then smiled at the Central Empire officer. "He's made a swell dad to me, Lieutenant. I hope I can become as good an actor as he is."

While she was talking, Nan's hand had quickly stolen under MacTavish's overcoat, and she slipped the revolver out of his back pocket. Then she turned sideways, and slid the gun into the pocket of her own overcoat.

The lieutenant's eyes were fixed upon MacTavish. "You do not look to me to be forty-six years old. You seem to be a much younger man. You do not seem to be old enough to be this boy's father."

MacTavish shrugged. "We actors must train ourselves to look young. You know how it is, Lieutenant—once you grow old in this business, you're done for."

"That is as may be," the lieutenant said coldly. "Be good enough to show me what it is that you have in your back pocket. I saw a bulge under your overcoat as you were walking."

The lieutenant's hand was resting significantly on the revolver in his own holster.

MacTavish grinned confidently. "My back pocket? You must be mistaken, Lieutenant. I have nothing in my back pocket."

He swung his coat around, turned and pulled the lining out of his hip pocket. "You see, it's empty."

The lieutenant was puzzled. "I distinctly saw a bulge under your coat," he persisted. "I think I will send you two in for further questioning to the District Commandant."

He raised a hand and signaled to a patrol of four troopers and a corporal who were passing. "Summon a car," he ordered the corporal, "and place these two under guard. You will take them to the District Commandant's office. You will say that Lieutenant Siegfried, of the Espionage Department, requests that they be questioned closely. I suspect that they are not what they appear to be."

The corporal saluted smartly, and ordered two of his men to go in search of a car.

SIEGE OF THE THOUSAND PATRIOTS

NAN CHRISTOPHER threw a hopeless glance at MacTavish, then stepped up close to the Central Empire officer. "But, Lieutenant, why do you insist on sending us in? We have done nothing wrong—" *

"Silence!" the lieutenant roared. "Do you dare to argue with

---

* AUTHOR'S NOTE: The names of Sergeant Aloysius MacTavish and Nan Christopher are well remembered by students of American history as prominent figures in the Purple Invasion. It might be well to recall how the Dictator of Balkaria launched his program of military preparedness and conquest which made him the most powerful ruler in Europe. His swift and ruthless thrusts reduced to vassalage one country after another until he fashioned the Central Empire, which embraced twenty-seven countries of Europe and Asia Minor. Then he marched his goose-stepping across Asia and made himself absolute master of that continent.

America had watched with a supine lack of interest, feeling that the geographical isolation of the United States made us safe from attack. But the Purple Emperor's vast fleet, carrying troops as well as the latest armaments and deadly gas, landed his huge military force in Canada and marched down through the New England States, occupying the eastern seaboard from Maine to Florida. With the American Government dispersed, only one man stood in the path of the Purple invader, as the American Defense Forces were beaten back beyond the Rocky Mountains.

Jimmy Christopher, known in the records of the United States Intelligence as Operator 5, organizer of the Minute Men of America in the Second War of Independence, continued the fight as second in command under Z-7, former chief of the Intelligence. Of the small band of loyal aides who risked their lives with Operator 5, Nan Christopher, his twin sister, and Sergeant

13

me? You both seem lacking in the respect due to an officer of the Central Empire. You have not saluted me, and the tone of your voice is not respectful enough." He grinned wickedly. "It will do you good to go through the course of questioning to which you will be subjected at the District Commandant's headquarters!"

Nan continued to protest, in a desperate, hopeless endeavor to avert the catastrophe which was threatening. "But our papers are in order—"

The lieutenant's face flushed with anger. "I ordered you to be silent! Have you not learned yet to obey?"

His big hand reached out, and seized Nan's coat lapels, yanked hard. Nan was almost carried off her feet. "I will show you," the lieutenant shouted, "proper respect for a Central Empire officer—"

He never finished, for MacTavish suddenly lunged in, crashing a big, hard fist to the Purple officer's jaw. The lieutenant's head was snapped back, and he staggered, still clutching the front of Nan's coat and shirt. The coat came open, and the shirt ripped.

But MacTavish noticed nothing. The fury of his anger sent him driving in at the officer, and his fists battered the other to the ground before the corporal and the two troopers of the patrol were able to leap upon him. They pinned his arms, dragged him off the officer.

The lieutenant picked himself up from the ground, his small,

MacTavish of the Royal Canadian Mounted Police were among the most daring and resourceful.

14

piggish eyes fixed not upon MacTavish, but upon Nan Christopher. The man's jaw was swelling swiftly, and his left eye was puffing up. Also, there were two long, blue bruises upon his left cheek.

But he paid no attention to these. His lips were twisted into a thick smile, and his eyes were fixed gloatingly upon the soft, rounded skin of Nan Christopher's breasts, which had been exposed by the tearing of the shirt.

Quickly she pulled the coat about her; but it was too late. While MacTavish struggled futilely in the grip of the two troopers, the lieutenant pushed his face close to Nan.

"So it is a girl, eh?—pretty girl! And she poses as a boy. This grows very interesting. I think that I will take you in to the Commandant's office—myself!"

CHAPTER 2
RETREAT, NEW STYLE

ON THAT same Sunday morning, far across the country, a small group of people stood upon a ridge of the Wasatch Mountains overlooking Strawberry Daniel Pass, which guarded the road to Salt Lake City. A cold snap, following an early snow, was reaching its icy tentacles over the length and the breadth of the land, and had encrusted the ridges of the mighty Wasatch Range with a glinting mantel of white ermine. Beyond the mountains, to the west, the rising sun was rippling across the waters of the Great Salt Lake, caressing its wavelets like a friend returning from a long journey.

But that small group of people had no eyes for the beauty of the mountains, nor for the sparkling spires of the Mormon Temple in Salt Lake City, which they could see from where they stood. The group consisted of two men, a young woman, and a boy.

One of those men was Jimmy Christopher, known in the records of the United States Intelligence as Operator 5. The older man who stood beside him was Z-7, formerly the Chief of all the United States Intelligence Units, but now actively in command of the American Defense Force.

Z-7 and Operator 5 were looking out over the limitless plains of Utah, which spread eastward toward the Green River. Jimmy Christopher, peering through his telescopic field glasses, could see endless lines of American troops moving toward them, to take up new positions in the Wasatch Mountains.

Those American troops had been dislodged from the Continental Divide far to the east, only a short while before. The Central Empire hosts had driven them back, and now they were forced to move the line of defense to this point. Long columns of weary marching Americans spread across the plains, appearing to be nothing more than long, wriggling worms upon the terrain far below.

As Jimmy Christopher moved his telescope from one point to another, the panorama that spread out before him was one of hopelessness. The dull, deep rumbling of enemy artillery came constantly to his ears. Spurts of dust were visible on the plain below, where the shells from the Central Empire guns kicked up the earth in huge sprays that resembled miniature geysers

The lieutenant's grasp on Nan's coat loosened as MacTavish drove his fist to the man's chin.

from up here. The retreating Americans were being subjected to a continual drum fire from the enemy artillery; and when a shell struck, Operator 5 could see the small, worm-like figures of the American soldiers scatter precipitately for safety. The enemy guns were miles away, yet they were harrying the rear guard of the American Defense Force. Soon they would move up within range of the Wasatch Mountains.

And then—retreat.

Retreat—or annihilation. That seemed to be the only choice for the American defenders. And another retreat would force them into the ocean.

Wearily, Operator 5 handed the field glass to Z-7. "Look at that, Chief! The enemy guns are cutting our men down, and we haven't a gun to answer with. There isn't a single battery in the American Defense Force that can equal the range of the Central Empire guns!"

Z-7 took the glass silently, and swept it over the plain. Jimmy Christopher turned to the other two people in the group, Diane Elliot and Tim Donovan. Diane Elliot's chestnut hair glinted in the sunlight. She wore a long army overcoat and a trench helmet. Her young, softly modeled features reflected the freshness and vigor, the honesty and the courage which had so endeared her to Operator 5. It was she who had fought by his side through all those dark days of the Purple Invasion when the Central Empire was trampling ruthlessly across the country and there seemed to be nothing left but death.

Weariness gripped her.

The events of the last few weeks had left their mark in her drooping figure and haunted eyes.

She had one arm around the shoulders of young Tim Donovan, whose freckled face and infectious grin had bolstered up the courage of herself as well as of Jimmy Christopher during the trying days of the past seven months.*

Diane met Jimmy Christopher's gaze bravely. "Jimmy!" she exclaimed. "What about Nan and Sergeant MacTavish? Today

---

* Author's Note: Anyone familiar with this period in history will undoubtedly recognize the names of Diane Elliot and Tim Donovan. No account of the campaigns of the Purple Invasion could possibly omit them or refuse to assign to them the major importance to which they are entitled. It is all too true that many historians have been inclined to belittle the part which they played in eventually preserving America from foreign domination. The reason for this may be attributed to the extreme reticence of Operator 5 and all of his little loyal band. They consistently allowed other to take credit for the things which they themselves accomplished, and never bothered to expose the petty lies and half truths by which ambitious men sought to further their own interests. Those who read these chronicles will for the first time learn the truth about the great part played by Operator 5, his sister Nan Christopher, Z-7, Diane Elliot, Tim Donovan, and those others of Operator 5's band who almost daily risked their lives in America's Second War of Independence. Diane Elliot had made her own place in the world as the star woman reported of the Amalgamated Press. Her fondest hope was the some day peace would come to America, and that Operator 5 would then case to be a number in the Intelligence Service and become Jimmy Chris-

is the day they were to contact Mayor Lacord in New York. We should have heard from them by this time—"

Her words were almost drowned by a sudden increased crescendo of booming thunder from the east. Jimmy Christopher swung around, in time to glimpse a sight of death and destruction on the plains below. New enemy batteries must have come into position, for the whole terrain was being virtually deluged by a rain of high explosive shells. It was as if a curtain of fire had suddenly been laid down upon the retreating Americans. WITH THE glass glued to his eye, Z-7 exclaimed hoarsely: "Good God, Jimmy, they must have brought those new guns of theirs to bear on us. They're wiping out our men."

Z-7 handed the glass to Jimmy, and covered his face with his hand. "It's murder, Jimmy," he groaned. "And we can't fight back. If half our men get through into the protection of these moun-

topher, the man—and her husband. But until that day arrived she insisted on sharing the risks to which he subjected himself.

As for the boy, Tim Donovan, he was scarcely beyond his middle teens. Two years before, as a hungry little newsboy, it had fallen to his lot to stand between Operator 5 and death. From that night on, Operator 5 had taken the lad under his wing, and taught him a hundred different things that no boy of his age could hope to know. Operator 5 had taught Tim Donovan to shoot, to fly, to drive a car, to operate a wireless key—in short, he had given the boy a complete education to equip him for service in the Intelligence Department. And Tim Donovan had rewarded all of Jimmy Christopher's care with quick-witted intelligence of practical use to Jimmy Christopher time and again.

tains, we'll be lucky. And we haven't the ammunition or the guns to cover their retreat."

Operator 5's eyes were cold and gray. His voice, though he spoke loudly, was almost indistinguishable above the deafening din of the enemy artillery. "The terrible part of it is, Chief, that those guns of theirs are being forged

in our own Pittsburgh steel mills. The enemy have rebuilt those mills, and they are using the forced labor of our own civilians to make cannon and ammunition. I hear that they have even captured Franklin Ransom, our foremost scientist and metallurgist."

Z-7's mouth snapped into a tight line. "What! Ransom captured? What about his new discovery—*ransomite?*"

Diane Elliot and Tim Donovan came close, and Diane exclaimed: "Did they get the formula for ransomite?"

Jimmy Christopher nodded somberly. "They caught Ransom working his way across the country with the formula. He was trying to reach our lines. They took him back a prisoner, and they've got him chained in the steel mill, working out the practical application of the formula. I hear they've already produced some ransomite, and it's successful. It's a lightweight alloy of steel, that will resist almost incredible pressure and stress. They have already made some big guns which they call 'Black Lightning.' It's a twenty-nine inch gun, and it's so light that it can be transported on an ordinary railroad flat car. It's equipped with a special track, to take up the recoil."

Jimmy Christopher pointed down across the plateau. "See those men dying down there? See those big shells exploding? They're being fired from the new guns. When they move those guns up within range of the Wasatch Mountains, what chance will we have of holding even this position?"

"My God!" Z-7 said almost under his breath. "If they've got the secret of ransomite, we haven't a chance in the world. They can turn out enough of those guns to smash every one of our coast cities!"

The four of them stood in a close group, watching with taut emotion the destruction that was taking place on the plain below. Thousands of men were dying before their eyes, and there was nothing they could do about it. Here and there they could see a column of American soldiers who had fought through the blazing curtain of drumfire, and who were racing toward the mountains. Army trucks kicked up gray clouds of dust as they sped westward, and the fleeing soldiers leaped up on those trucks. But fully half of them were caught in the barrage.

Z-7 said wearily: "We can't go on like this. Perhaps it would be better to surrender, after all, the way the Board of Governors wanted us to do. This is just slaughter!"

Young Tim Donovan broke into harsh laughter. "Surrender? After what we've been through to keep the fight going? Nix, Z-7!"

Z-7 said quickly to Tim Donovan: "Run back to the field telephone. 'Phone staff headquarters. Tell them to direct Colonel

Fitzhugh to move his batteries west to a position just outside the town of Kimball. Have them send up a flight of scout planes to locate those new enemy batteries. We've got to silence them!"

Tim Donovan nodded, raced back toward a dugout where the field telephone was located, about fifty yards back. In the meantime, Z-7, Operator 5 and Diane watched helplessly while the men on the plain below were being slaughtered. In a few moments Tim returned, his face white.

"It's no use, Z-7," the lad gasped. "Colonel Fitzhugh's battery is out of ammunition. The only ammunition we have is for the light guns, and they couldn't even touch the enemy artillery. I told staff headquarters to ask for volunteer bombers to go out and try to *strafe* the enemy artillery. But there's not much chance of their getting over the enemy line."

Z-7's face was haggard. "It means that this retreat will have to keep up. We might be able to hold the Wasatch Range here for a few days, but they'll shell us out of it, as sure as shooting!"

Jimmy Christopher put a hand on Z-7's arm. "Look, Chief. The situation here is practically hopeless. If they keep pushing us back, there'll be no place to retreat, but into the Pacific Ocean. Well, since we can't retreat—" his voice suddenly took on a note of cold resolution—"let's attack!"

Z-7 looked at him queerly. "What do you mean—attack? We can't pit flesh and blood against twenty-nine inch guns—"

"I don't mean that, Chief. We'll attack from within. Let me take a hundred men. I'll go through the enemy line, and try to cripple their bases of supplies and manufacture."

"You're crazy," Z-7 said. "How could you get through—"

Jimmy Christopher said eagerly: "We've got enough Central Empire prisoners from whom we can borrow uniforms. We'll outfit our men as officers and privates of the Purple Army. We've got half a dozen captured motor lorries. I'll take three, and work east along the Great Lakes region, and Diane can take the other three and work along the southern route, through St. Louis and Dayton. I can get up enough credentials to show that the men are bona fide Central Empire officers and soldiers, who have been relieved from active service at the front, and ordered east. We can communicate with our undercover men in each of the cities by amateur radio, and have them meet us at a prearranged spot.

"We'll detach two or three men at each city, and leave instructions for organizing a rebellion to take place at a given signal. If we can arrange uprisings in scattered parts of the occupied territory for a particular day, Rudolph will have to rush troops to those cities, and he will leave only skeleton forces at the places where there are no rebellions. One of those places will be Pittsburgh, and I'll be there.

"When the troops have been moved out of the Pittsburgh area, I'll see what I can do about destroying the steel mills there. I may even have an opportunity to rescue Franklin Ransom."

Z-7 hesitated, and Operator 5 went on pleadingly: "It's our only chance, Chief. If we can stop the production of the big guns, and if we can get Ransom's secret of ransomite, there may be a chance for us."

"By God!" Z-7 breathed, "It's just mad enough to succeed. And there's nothing else left for us to do." Suddenly he stretched out his hand, his eyes flashing. "Go ahead, Jimmy. And may God go with you!"

CHAPTER 3
DESTINY IN FETTERS

A SMOKY murk lay over the city of Pittsburgh like a gray pall. It emanated from a hundred smoke-stacks in a hundred busily humming steel plants. Great converters sent a flare of brilliant vermilion up into the night. Huge drop-forging plants clanged in majestic competition to the whining of dynamos.

And in all these hundreds of plants which had been erected from the ruins of a devastated Pittsburgh, captive Americans worked in chains, sweating in the heat of the Bessemer shops to produce the sinews of war by which their conquerors hoped to beat the rest of America to its—knees. In the mines, other captive Americans burrowed deep into the earth for the raw material with which to supply the factories. And train after train rumbled into the city bearing loads of pig-iron to be converted into steel implements of warfare.

The whole of Allegheny County had been placed under martial law. Gray-clad, steel-helmeted troops of the Central Empire guarded every road and every approach into the county. Here, in the heart of the section where armaments were being manufactured, the Central Empire had laid down laws for civilians more strict than anywhere else. Americans had been brought into Allegheny County in herds, like cattle, chained to one another, and put to work in the steel mills and in the mines. Other thousands were engaged in the construction of new buildings in the heart of the city, to replace those structures which had been destroyed by the intensive bombardment of the Purple artillery at the time Pittsburgh had been captured.

Aside from this forced labor, no Americans were permitted within the bounds of Allegheny County. Colonel Goermann, the Commandant of the Occupied Territory of Pennsylvania, was taking no chances on any abortive uprising among the conquered people. All those Americans employed in the plant where the big guns were being made were never permitted to leave the shops.

They worked, ate and slept in the same place. If any secrets were known to them, they would never have an opportunity to communicate them to their friends on the other side of the Rockies.

One building in particular was especially well guarded by the enemy troops. This was the new experimental building, which had been erected on the site of old Fort Pitt at the junction of the Allegheny and Monongahela Rivers, right in the heart of Pittsburgh.

It was a long, rambling structure only one story high, but it spread out over an area of almost four square blocks. At the north end of the building, overlooking the Allegheny River, Colonel Goermann had made his headquarters. The remainder of the building was devoted to experimental work, and in one of the great chambers at the south end, an old man sat on a wooden bench.

His face was gaunt, and his eyes burned with a constant hatred for his captors. His ankles were chained to a steel girder running along the floor close to the wall. Before him was spread a huge workbench upon which lay hundreds of samples of forged steel, each one of them labeled.

This man was Franklin Ransom, the inventor of ransomite.

His white hair topped a high intellectual forehead. He sat hunched over the work bench, forgetful of his shackled ankles, engrossed in a batch of blueprints that lay spread out before him.

Beside him sat another American, a younger man. This was Henry Daws, who had been Ransom's assistant throughout his extensive experimental work.

RANSOM WAS dictating rapidly, and Daws was sketching from his dictation. There was an arched doorway at the far end of the room, through which Ransom could look out into the other portions of the building. Out there he could see hundreds of other shackled Americans working at miniature open hearths. Those men were producing the various alloys of steel on which Ransom was working. Those alloys were destined, if successful, to be used in the manufacture of even greater guns and tanks.

Franklin Ransom abruptly put down his pencil, and stared gloomily out through the arched doorway. He said bitterly to his assistant: "Henry, I think we've got the formula for ransomite three. If I gave it to Goermann, it means that the Central Empire will be able to manufacture a Big Bertha even greater

27

than those used in the World War, yet one that can be transported without difficulty. Do you understand what that means, Henry?"

Young Daws stopped his sketching, and looked up. "Good God, Mr. Ransom, we can't do it. Let's destroy these sketches—"

He stopped, letting his voice drift off without finishing the sentence. His eyes met those of Ransom, and each knew what was in the mind of the other.

Slowly Ransom nodded. "Yes," the scientist breathed, "it's hard to be a hero sometimes. Our wives and children are in the hands of the Central Empire. We either do this work for them, or we see our children disemboweled by the bayonets of those troopers." He shuddered. "It's a terrible choice—we have it in our hands to kill our children or kill our country."

His gaze wandered to the guard of six troopers who stood at attention along the wall, with fixed bayonets. In the other rooms there were other troopers—enough to quell the slightest sign of rebellion among these forced workers.

"If there were only some means of escaping—and of taking along our families!" His shoulders sagged hopelessly. "Henry, we're cowards. The old Greeks and Romans would willingly have sacrificed their wives and children for the sake of their country. But we—we have been softened by two thousand years of civilization."

Henry Daws put a hand on the old man's arm. He whispered: "Couldn't we work out some sort of flaw or defect for the manufacture of ransomite three—something that would cause a structural weakness in the guns—"

Ransom shook his head. "The Central Empire scientists check up very carefully on everything that we do. They're following these experiments closely. The minute they discover the principle behind my formula, they will go ahead with their experiments themselves, and they won't need me anymore. They'd be quick to discover anything that would tend to weaken the alloy."

Ransom felt Henry Daw's hand stiffen on his arm. He glanced toward the doorway, and his eyes darkened with veiled hatred as he saw Colonel Goermann enter.

Goermann was a chunky, heavy-set man with a very broad nose and contrastingly thin lips. The Colonel was wearing no hat, and his large round head showed completely bald under the powerful electric light. That immense, bald head of his looked almost obscene in its nakedness as the Colonel strode up close to Ransom's work table. The thin gash that was his mouth twisted into a sardonic grin.

"Goot evening, Herr Ransom. Your experiments—they go well?"

The scientist glared up at him from the bench to which he was shackled. "They go too well, damn you. I—"

Still smiling twistedly, Goermann reached quickly over and slapped Ransom's face sharply with his pudgy hand. The blow was like the crack of a whip. A great red splotch appeared on Ransom's cheek.

"You will learn to talk more respectfully, my goot frient!" Goermann straightened, continued to smile.

Young Henry Daws half rose in his seat, clenching his hands. His eyes lanced hatred at the chunky Central Empire Colonel.

Goermann's hand slipped toward the butt of the holstered revolver at his side. He said softly: "Sit down, Daws—or I will shoot you dead and leave you shackled to your bench. Your body will rot here and your frient, the goot Mr. Ransom, will be compelled to smell it!"

White-faced with anger, Daws restrained himself with a visible effort, sank slowly back into his seat. He had seen Goermann shoot others in just that way, without a moment's hesitation. He knew the Colonel would do it again.

GOERMANN TURNED back to Ransom. "You were saying, my goot frient, that the experiments were going well. You expect to have ransomite three ready for manufacture soon?"

Ransom hesitated, then said reluctantly: "I think I'm on the right track. I should be finished in a week—"

Goermann leaned over, resting his finger-tips on the work bench. "You will be ready in less than a week, my goot frient. You will be ready in three days. My imperial master, the Emperor Rudolph, wishes to celebrate his coronation on Sunday with the news that we are ready to begin making the big guns from your new metal. That Sunday is three days from today. You will have ransomite three ready for manufacture by then."

"But it can't be done," Ransom protested. "There are at least thirty more alloy tests to be made—"

"Nevertheless," Goermann said coldly, "you will have ransomite three finished by Sunday!"

He swung around, raised his hand in signal to a sergeant who stood in the arched doorway. The sergeant grinned, saluted, and swung around smartly. He disappeared, only to return in a

A black moustache in
the Imperial tradition
gave Operator 5 the look
of a Purple officer.

moment, followed by four troopers. Each pair of troopers had a small child between them. The first was a curly-headed boy of five. The second pair of troopers held a little girl of seven. Both children were obviously frightened by the hard-faced Central Empire soldiers who held them with painful grips on their little arms.

Ransom's face whitened, and his knuckles grew taught as he gripped the edge of his work bench. "Bobbie! Marie!" he choked out.

The sergeant advanced and saluted smartly again. "The Ransom children, at your orders, my Colonel," he reported.

Goermann's wicked smile did not fade from his chunky countenance. He rapped out a swift order in the guttural language of the Central Empire, and the sergeant faced the squad of troopers lined up against the far wall, repeated the command. The squad shouldered arms, marched briskly around until they were lined up facing the two children. At another order from the sergeant they grounded their arms, then raised the rifles, presenting the points of the bayonets at the stomachs of the two little children. Bobbie and Marie shrank from those glittering points, but they were held ruthlessly by their captors.

Ransom shouted hoarsely: "Wait! Wait! No, no. Stop them, Goermann!"

Goermann said slowly: "You—er—think that you will be able to have ransomite three ready for production by Sunday?"

"Yes, yes. Anything, anything. I'll—have it ready."

Goermann's eyes flickered with triumph. "See that you do.

32

Otherwise, my goot frient, you will witness the disemboweling of your two so-sweet children!"

Swiftly he issued a series of orders, and the troopers withdrew their bayonets, returned to the wall. The sergeant saluted once more, and led the two captive children out of the room. Little Bobbie struggled ineffectively in the grip of the two troopers, attempting to run to his father. Tears were streaming from his eyes as they dragged him out, but he uttered not a word. Little Marie, on the other hand, began to cry, and her heartrending sobs dinned against Ransom's tortured ears until her poor little voice was smothered by the big hand of one of the troopers across her mouth.

Ransom dropped his head on his arms upon the work bench. Henry Daws sat rigid, his eyes speaking their sympathy for his chief.

Goermann smiled cynically, turned on his heel and strode from the room.

For a long minute there was silence. Then Ransom slowly raised his head, heaved a deep sigh. "Come, Henry. We must go to work. God forgive me, I'm going to make ransomite three for those fiends. I—I'm only human. I—I'd do anything to keep those bayonets from twisting in the bowels of Bobbie and Marie!"

He looked out through the barred windows toward the south where the night was being made into a garish phantasmagoria of light, funneling from the long slender towers of the blast furnaces working twenty-four hours a day to convert American ore into iron and steel for the destruction of Americans. The great steel mills of Pittsburgh and the long rows of coal sheds and slag piles were clearly visible, limned into bold relief by the flaring light of the furnaces.

Ransom closed his eyes hard for a moment, then turned viciously to the task of working out the proper formula for ransomite three. And in the outer room beyond the ached doorway, those other Americans who were shackled to the floor before the flaming portholes of the miniature blast furnaces were emptying the seething, writhing molten iron from the open hearths into ladles to be transported by the small overhead traveling cranes into the rows of ingot molds on the other side. Sputtering steel overflowed, and men died, screaming with the agony of hideous burns which they could not avoid because of their shackles.

Stolid Central Empire guards watched the injured men, not even bothering to move to their help. The flesh and bone of living Americans were almost literally being cast into those molds which were to form the great guns destined to blast the American Defense Forces out of their position in the Wasatch Mountains. And these men worked dully, hopelessly, looking forward to nothing for themselves, but hoping that by their toil and by the sweat of their brow they would preserve their women and children from torture and death.*

---

* AUTHOR'S NOTE: It is a matter of record that 3,450 American men died in the steel mills of Allegheny County during the six months that they were under operation by the Central Empire. Many historians have hesitated to touch at any great length upon this black page of the Purple Invasion.

SIEGE OF THE THOUSAND PATRIOTS

This is no doubt due to the fact that it is a painful thing to recall the misery, humiliation, torture, agony and death to which our citizens were subjected under the Forced Labor Draft Laws of the Central Empire. All the ordinary precautions the great steel companies of the United States had taken to protect the lives and limbs of the working men in their shops went by the board when the Central Empire took possession. Life was cheap to Rudolph, and he did not count it at all as against his need for steel and iron. It is recorded that of the 3,450 casualties, 1,400 men perished from first degree burns resulting from contact of the living body with molten steel. Almost another thousand were mangled to death by defective machinery which was kept in operation until it fell to pieces. The rest died of starvation, ill-treatment or slaughter by the ruthless guards. And just as Colonel Goermann had threatened, their bodies were left to rot in the chains that shackled them unless it became necessary to replace them with other workmen. In that case their pitiful remains were often hurled into the Monongahela River without so much as a prayer.

If these forced draft workers appear to the modern reader to have been cowardly and supine, it must be borne in mind that every one of them had been selected only after the Central Empire task masters were assured that they had their hands on the man's family. Just as they did with the workers on the coronation arch and St. Patrick's Cathedral in New York, they compelled these men to work like beasts of burden in order to save their families. It would take a man with a heart of steel to deliberately permit his wife and children to be disemboweled before his very eyes when it was within his power to prevent it—even though that act of prevention meant danger to his country. Let us not, therefore, judge them too harshly—especially in

CHAPTER 4
THE DUEL

THREE MOTOR lorries were driving swiftly into Chicago along Highway 14 from Minneapolis. The men in those three lorries all wore the uniforms of the Central Empire. Strangely, however, they seemed to belong to various oddly assorted branches of the Imperial Army. Another peculiar thing about them was that there seemed to be more officers than privates. There were a number of first and second lieutenants, and many corporals and sergeants.

They were from the infantry, the artillery, the engineers, the flying corps, the quartermaster's department; and there were even two corporals of the Central Empire Military Police.

The side of the hood of each of the motor lorries was duly emblazoned with the severed head and crossed broadswords of the Central Empire; and upon the windshield of each truck was pasted the usual certificates of the General Staff of the Imperial Army without which no vehicle was permitted to travel behind the lines. This certificate stated that the occupants of the lorry were proceeding by the eastern seaboard by order of the General Staff, and were to be granted every facility in their travels.

The driver of the leading truck was an extremely youthful individual whose head was bandaged in such a way as to hide the distinctive freckles upon his face. But his pert little

view of the courage and fortitude which these men later exhibited, as will be related in a subsequent chapter.

pug-nose showed between the folds of the bandages, as did his lively, dancing eyes.

Beside him sat the commander of this small caravan—a well-built young man in the uniform of a major of the Imperial Hussars. If one had been puzzled by the apparent youth of this officer, he would have been restrained from asking impertinent questions by the sight of the fierce, black moustache which the young major sported in the best manner of the Central Empire.

As the trucks rolled down Higgins Road, then swung into Milwaukee Avenue in the heart of Chicago, the men within those trucks seemed to have not a care in the world. They were harmonizing in voices that were just loud enough not to be heard above the sound of their motors. But if any subject of his Imperial Majesty, Rudolph I, had heard what they were singing, that subject would have been duly astounded. For they were not singing the great national anthem of the Central Empire which begins:

> By the grace of Rudolph and God
> We march on conquered sod....

Instead, that strangely assorted band of men in Central Empire uniforms was singing:

> Oh, the Dutch compan-ee
> Was the best compan-ee

That ever came over the sea!

As the driver of the small cavalcade swung from Milwaukee Avenue into Wacker Drive, heading toward the lake, the voices of the singers in the leading truck rose a trifle. The mustached young major turned in his seat and growled: "Listen, you fellows, cut that out now. You'll get the whole Purple Army down on us if you keep it up."

One of the men inside the truck said: "Okay, Operator 5. We didn't think we were singing so loud. We'll pipe down."

The major chuckled. "You don't have to pipe down altogether. You can sing as much as you like—as long as you sound like true subjects of his Imperial Majesty."

One of the troopers in the rear of the truck had signaled over the tail-board to those in the following trucks to quiet down, and now the singing ceased entirely. But in a moment it began again. This time, however, they began to sing the National Anthem of the Purple Empire—as lustily as if they believed every word of it:

By the grace of Rudolph and God
We march on conquered sod.
We flaunt the flag of our sovereign lord
In the face of the fleeing horde.
When the might of the Purple Empire
Marches on with sword and fire
No man shall be found so high

But must bow his head or die!*

Verse after verse of the cruel, triumphant Central Empire Anthem these men sang as the three motor lorries swung out of Wacker Drive and turned south into Michigan Avenue, along the lake front.

THE YOUTHFUL driver of the first truck, said to the major: "Gee Jimmy, that moustache of yours is sure the goods.

---

* AUTHOR'S NOTE: There has been much discussion by those who are interested in the little known sidelights of history as to the authorship of the Purple National Anthem. A number of different versions are extant. Some contend that the words of the original version written by Maximilian I, Rudolph's father, when he led the troops of the Central Empire against the Soviet Union. It was when Maximilian I, founder of the Central Empire, after conquering the countries of Western Europe marched across Russia with practically no opposition, that the Purple National Anthem, as it is now known, was first sung by Maximilian's troops. There is a story to the effect that Maximilian compelled that well known Viennese composer, Kurt Kreutz, to compose the stirring music of the anthem, and later ordered Kreutz's execution so that the composer should never do another piece of music after having created the Purple National Anthem. Furthermore, it was forbidden to print or to publish this anthem anywhere that the Purple Emperor ruled. I am proud to say that after a good deal of research in the secret archives of the Purple Empire I have been able to discover the original manuscript of the song as composed by Kurt Kreutz, and I am happy to publish one page here for the benefit of those of our readers who are interested.

But what would you do if it fell off while you were talking to some Central Empire general?"

Jimmy Christopher laughed. "It can't fall off, Tim. It's glued on with a special make-up paste. If anybody pulled it hard enough, my skin would come away with it, but the paste wouldn't give." He was about to ease his position on the seat when he suddenly stiffened.

"Look out, Tim!" he exclaimed.

A long gray staff car with the insignia of the Imperial Army on the radiator had come swinging out of Congress Street, making a sharp left turn into Michigan Avenue, almost directly in their path.

Tim Donovan stepped down hard on the brake, and twisted the wheel to the right, to avoid being hit. But the staff car was moving so fast that its fender crashed into the left front wheel of the motor lorry. Little damage was done to either car, as both drivers had stepped down on their brakes.

But the driver of the staff car flung open the door and came storming out. Jimmy Christopher's heart sank as he saw that the driver of this car was not a chauffeur, but was attired in the full uniform of a brigadier general of the Imperial Army.

The man was in his forties, florid-faced, and drunk as a lord. Two other officers alighted from the car behind the brigadier general. One was a colonel, the other a captain. These two were also well under the weather.

A number of Central Empire troopers and officers who had been walking in the street stopped to watch the scene. The general wobbled over toward the truck, and fumbled at his

holster for the revolver which rested there. At the same time
he looked up toward Tim Donovan and barked: "Come down
here, you mangy cur! How dare you get in the way of the automobile of Brigadier General Count von Zuppert? Come down
here and I will shoot you through the head!"

He had his revolver half way out now, and was making an
ineffectual attempt to clamber up on the running board of the
truck, alongside the cab. The colonel and the captain who had
been riding with him gave him their drunken support, trying
to push him up toward the driver's seat.

Tim Donovan threw a hasty glance at Operator 5. They both
realized the danger of the situation. In the Imperial Army the
authority of a high ranking officer over the life of a private
trooper was unquestioned. If this Brigadier General von
Zuppert took it into his head to murder Tim Donovan, no one
would question him. It was part of the discipline of the Purple
Army, and it had worked to perfection with the bovine peas-
ants whom Rudolph had conscripted for his armies. They were
by nature cruel and lustful themselves; and the only discipline
they could understand was the discipline which carried with it
the threat of instant death. Therefore, Rudolph had given to his
ranking officers the right to inflict death at their discretion as a
punishment for any infraction of the rules or for any disrespect
to a superior officer.

Jimmy Christopher knew this very well, and he knew that
there was no way of saving the life of Tim Donovan if von
Zuppert wanted to kill him for his own satisfaction. There was
no law to which the Brigadier General would be answerable,

and in his present drunken state the innately sadistic nature of the man was taking free range.

He had his revolver out now, and was shouting thickly: "Come down here, you swine! Come down, or I will shoot you out of that seat!"

Tim Donovan, his face covered by the bandage, whispered out of the corner of his mouth: "What'll I do, Jimmy? Should we make a break for it? We could drive through these guys—"

"No, no, Tim. It would ruin all our plans. This drunken devil

would turn the military police out after us, and we'd be picked up eventually. Sit tight."

Von Zuppert was already raising his gun to shoot, when Operator 5 suddenly pushed along the seat and climbed over Tim Donovan, placing himself between the lad and the general's gun.

Von Zuppert's blood-shot eyes focused on Jimmy's uniform, and he frowned, but did not shoot.

"Who are you?" he sputtered.

Jimmy Christopher smiled disarmingly, and leaped down from the truck. "My dear General!" he exclaimed. "I am desolated. I am deeply mortified. What a fool of a driver I have! I hope he has done no damage to your car. I shall have him punished severely!"

Von Zuppert glowered at him. "I do not know you," he said. "Who are you? What are you doing with these trucks?"

Jimmy Christopher snapped to attention, and saluted sharply. Inwardly he was rejoicing. He had already succeeded in diverting von Zuppert's attention from Tim Donovan. "I am Major von Innsbruck, of the Nineteenth Imperial Hussars, my General. I am proceeding east with a picked group of men selected from various branches of the Imperial Service. We are reporting for special duty."

The Brigadier General hesitated. Jimmy added shrewdly: "I have orders to report in person to the Emperor. I assure you, my General, that I shall see to it that my driver is properly punished after we have reached our destination. But I will call to your attention that his Imperial Majesty would be greatly displeased were he to learn that a matter of routine had interfered with our journey."

Von Zuppert lowered his gun, doubtfully. The bold assurance of this young major caused him to have some qualms, even in his drunken condition.

For he realized that Rudolph had as much power over him as he had over a private soldier; and that if this contingent of troopers were proceeding east at Rudolph's orders, the Emperor might be highly angered at anyone who stopped them. It was one thing to shoot down a defenseless private in the army; but it was altogether a different matter to kill anyone who was traveling on special orders from the Emperor.

JIMMY MIGHT have gotten away with it, except that the colonel who had been in the staff car with von Zuppert now stepped forward and whispered in the general's ear. His voice carried so that Jimmy could hear what he said:

"Let us look at this man's credentials, General. I have never heard of a Major von Innsbruck in the Imperial Hussars. As a matter of fact, my brother-in-law is with the Nineteenth Imperial Hussars, and I would certainly have heard him mention the name, for he has talked with me about all the officers in the regiment at one time or another."

Operator 5 sighed. Above all things he had wanted to avoid

trouble. They had traveled across two-thirds of the continent already, dropping off one or two men in each large city to sow the seed of rebellion, and to arrange for a universal uprising at a given signal. Nothing must be permitted to stop this cavalcade from continuing its passage across the country and finally carrying out the objective that Operator 5 had set for himself.

But these three drunken officers were likely to cause their destruction.

The men inside the three motor lorries were growing restless. They would never permit von Zuppert and his two companions to harm Tim Donovan. Jimmy knew all those men well. He knew that if danger threatened they would act without orders. They were a reckless, courageous lot, as was evidenced by the fact that they had all volunteered to join this expedition across enemy territory, disguised as Central Empire officers and soldiers. Even now Operator 5 could hear them stirring inside the trucks, could hear the cocking of revolvers. They were preparing to put up a fight right here and now, surrounded as they were by the enemy.

There could be only one end to such an adventure—death or capture for all of them.

Jimmy Christopher's mind raced quickly, desperately, over all the possibilities of action in this particular situation. His eyes moved keenly from Brigadier General von Zuppert to the colonel who was whispering in his ear, and to the captain who was standing only a foot or two away, also swaying on his feet.

The colonel continued persistently: "Of course, General, I do not suspect that this young whippersnapper of a major is an enemy in disguise. But I think he ought to be disciplined. I don't like these youngsters who attain high rank in the army by reason of their family connections. Let us chastise him, General—"

Von Zuppert nodded in sudden agreement. "You are right, Colonel Goetz. I will place this young whippersnapper under arrest—"

A small crowd of Central Empire officers had gathered about them, laughing and making sarcastic comments under their breath, and throwing commiserating glances at the unfortunate young major who was incurring the wrath of the Brigadier General.

And in a flash of inspiration the solution of the problem came to Jimmy Christopher.

He recalled abruptly the fact that all commissioned officers in the forces of the Central Empire were considered to be of the same social caste; and that an officer must be, above all, a gentleman—according to the standards of the Central Empire. Dueling among officers and gentlemen was considered a fashionable thing among these autocratic military men. To refuse a challenge to a duel was enough to cause any officer to lose caste—no matter how high his rank. Jimmy saw that Colonel Goetz's face bore a sabre mark across the left cheek—an honorable scar among the dueling gentlemen of the Central Empire.

Jimmy Christopher glanced up at the cab of the leading lorry, and saw that Tim Donovan had drawn his own automatic. The boy's eyes were bright with excitement and anger. No doubt, the other men in the lorries were also under acute tension. Any one of them might precipitate a conflict at any moment, and all would be lost.

So Operator 5 acted with swiftness.

He stepped close to the two officers, raised his right hand and brought it lightly across Colonel Goetz's face in a backhanded slap. Goetz's face flushed angrily, and his hand went to the hilt of the sabre at his belt.

Jimmy Christopher said coldly: "I could not help hearing what you whispered to General von Zuppert. Your words and your tone are deliberately insulting to an officer and a gentleman, Colonel Goetz, I demand immediate satisfaction!"

THE OFFICERS who had gathered around them burst into excited comments and conversation. Jimmy could hear snatches of words here and there: "What a fool to challenge the foremost duelist of the Empire! Goetz will cut him to pieces. Why, the Colonel has won forty-two duels, and he never spares an adversary. The man is committing suicide to challenge Goetz!"

Goetz's anger had suddenly given way to a sort of veiled cunning. The sight of this youngster deliberately offering himself as a sacrifice to the Colonel's deadly sabre was almost too good to be true.

He licked his lips, and his eyes glowed meanly. "You—you desire satisfaction? You—challenge *me* to a duel?"

Jimmy Christopher said coldly: "How else do you interpret the blow I just gave you?"

Goetz breathed a deep sigh of satisfaction. "It is well," he breathed. "My sabre grows rusty from lack of use."

General von Zuppert had already lost all interest in Tim Donovan and in his desire to punish the lad. His little pig-eyes were sparkling in anticipation of the fun to come.

"Good!" he exclaimed. "A duel is the very thing. I shall enjoy myself immensely. As for seconds—"

"We do not need seconds," Jimmy Christopher said coldly. "If you will be good enough to give the signal for us to commence, General—"

Von Zuppert frowned. "You wish to fight here and now?"

"Here and now," Operator 5 repeated firmly. "When I am insulted, I do not rest until I have vindicated my honor."

A number of the disguised Americans from the three trucks had descended to the ground, and now they with the onlookers from the street formed a wide semi-circle around the small group. Tim Donovan remained in the truck, watching closely out of his bandage.

General von Zuppert glanced questioningly at Colonel Goetz. "It's a little irregular, Goetz—this dueling in the street without seconds. What say you?"

Goetz shrugged with an assumption of carelessness. "Since the gentleman demands immediate satisfaction, I am ready to give it to him. Why delay? It will be good sport."

Von Zuppert grinned. "Yes, yes. Good sport, indeed." He turned to Jimmy. "We will proceed at once. You will cross sabres and disengage when I drop my sword. Perhaps, Major von Innsbruck," he added softly, speaking to Jimmy, "you wish to make a will or last statement?"

Operator 5 smiled nonchalantly, and twirled his moustache

with a flourish. "It will be unnecessary, my General. I do not expect to die."

Goetz laughed harshly. "Let us begin. We do not wish to waste too much time!"

"Right!" said Jimmy. They both drew their heavy sabres, raised them in the air in stiff salute. Von Zuppert drew his own sword, and said: "Now!"

Colonel Goetz and the bogus Major von Innsbruck crossed their sabres in the air, held them rigidly so, while Brigadier General von Zuppert touched his sword to their two blades at the point where they crossed.

A stir of interest and excitement ran through the onlookers. Many were sorry for the headstrong young major who was about to meet death at the hands of the famous duelist, Herman Goetz. Others were watching keenly for the blow that would finish the fight. The swordsmen had removed their overcoats, and the sharp wind, blowing almost in a gale from the lake, whipped against their faces and bodies, whining through the street.

General von Zuppert suddenly said: "Ready!" and dropped his sword.

IMMEDIATELY THE two duelists rasped the blades of their sabres one against the other as they sprang into fighting position. Goetz's sabre clashed against Jimmy's as he slashed with relentless blow after blow to break down Jimmy's guard.

The cold air crackled with sparks from the two blades. Goetz was a powerful man, and he fought in the traditional manner of the heavyweight cavalry duelists who believed in beating down his enemy's guard without giving him time to make a *riposte*.

Goetz had won forty-two duels with his slashing, vicious, headstrong manner of attack. His tactics kept an opponent forever parrying without an opportunity to make a thrust of his own. Within two minutes of fighting, Jimmy Christopher knew that he was matched with no unworthy opponent. For Goetz, in addition to the weight of his body and the strength of his wrists, displayed an amazing amount of skill as well as a thorough knowledge of the art of fencing. There was an assurance about this man, a deep feeling of self-confidence, which had been bred in him by his numerous victories.

Jimmy Christopher could see in the Colonel's eyes that the man would have no mercy for an opponent. He was fighting either to kill or to maim seriously. He was the type of duelist who took pleasure not so much in winning his duel as in crippling his enemy. A dozen times Goetz slashed viciously in an effort to beat down Jimmy Christopher's guard.

But Operator 5 was far from a novice at this business. Many years ago he had served an apprenticeship in the famous *salle d'armes* of Scherevesky, the greatest living master of fencing foils. Jimmy Christopher had become so proficient a pupil that Scherevesky had begged him to represent France at the International Fencing Matches. Jimmy had not accepted the offer, and Scherevesky in a rage had challenged his young student to a duel. That duel made fencing history, for Jimmy Christopher succeeded in touching his teacher three times, and each of those three times he could just as easily have delivered a mortal thrust.

Scherevesky had shaken his head in despair. His rage was forgotten in the contemplation of the supreme skill to which a pupil of his had attained. He begged and pleaded with Jimmy to enter the international competition. But Operator 5 never sought personal glory. He had sought to make himself proficient in fencing, as he had done in other walks of life, only for the purpose of increasing his usefulness in the career which he had chosen.

So now, Operator 5 could coolly evaluate his antagonist, and yet he felt no fears as to the outcome. Goetz slashed downward powerfully at Jimmy's shoulder.

The blow would have sliced Jimmy Christopher's arm off had he not parried it skillfully in *seconde*. Then he twisted sharply, and executed a swift lunge in *tierce*. Goetz had been carried slightly forward by his slashing blow, and Jimmy's recovery after the parry had been so spectacularly swift that the Colonel had no time to defend himself.

Jimmy Christopher's sabre reached its mark unerringly, piercing Goetz's throat

Blood spurted in a livid stream as Jimmy's sabre went through the man's neck. Goetz's eyes opened wide in terror, and a gurgling scream died in his throat. The sagging weight of his body dragged at Jimmy's sabre, and Operator 5 withdrew it swiftly. Goetz's dead body collapsed on the cold ground.

A low, involuntary cheer went up from the bystanders. The contest had lasted only five minutes, and the swift interplay of the weapons had been almost impossible to follow with the naked eye. Yet they had all seen enough to understand that this supposed Major von Innsbruck was a past master of the sabre.

Characteristically, there was no sympathy for the dead colonel. Just as in a prizefight, all the thoughts of the onlookers were for the victor. A dozen of the Central Empire officers swarmed around Jimmy Christopher, patting him on the back and shaking his hand. Goetz's body was almost trampled under their feet in their eagerness to congratulate this man who had in five minutes vanquished the victor of forty-two duels. Of course, many of these men had no doubt hated Goetz secretly but had refrained from expressing their opinion of him lest they incur his wrath. Now they were almost jubilant.

Brigadier General von Zuppert pushed drunkenly through the crowd.

Jimmy Christopher's hand tightened on the grip of his sabre.

Goetz had been the General's companion. Von Zuppert might be angry....

BUT THE Brigadier General was far from angry. All his rage against Tim Donovan was forgotten. Any friendship that might have existed between himself and Colonel Goetz was also forgotten. He was almost sputtering in his eagerness to congratulate Jimmy Christopher on the amazing victory. He threw his arms around Jimmy and hugged him.

Jimmy kept the disgust which he felt from showing on his face.

"My dear von Innsbruck!" Brigadier General von Zuppert exclaimed. "You were marvelous. Where did you acquire such skill? Why, man, you are the premier duelist of the Purple Army.

I shall take you to the Emperor in person. My friend, I beg you, give me some lessons in fencing!"

"It will give me great pleasure to do so, General," Jimmy Christopher told him.

"I shall be in New York on Sunday for the Emperor's coronation," von Zuppert went on. "You are going to New York?"

Jimmy nodded. "These men who are with me in the trucks have all been ordered to New York to participate in the coronation. They have been selected from among the men at the front as those being most worthy of imperial reward for bravery."

Von Zuppert patted Jimmy's arm. "That is good. I shall expect you to call upon me. Do not forget."

"Thank you, my General," Jimmy Christopher said modestly. "Now, about Colonel Goetz—"

"Never mind, never mind," von Zuppert said impatiently. "We will take care of the body. Go ahead, now, von Innsbruck. Go ahead with your men. But remember to look me up in New York."

Jimmy motioned to several of his men, and they pushed the general's staff car out of the way of the leading truck. Then they all got back into the lorries. Jimmy Christopher was compelled to shake hands with almost fifty of the enthusiastic officers who surrounded him. At last he broke away from them, mounted in the cab alongside Tim Donovan, and said tersely: "Go ahead, Tim. Let's get out of here before he changes his mind!"

Tim Donovan had already shifted gears. He sent the truck rolling down Michigan Avenue, followed by the second and third trucks, amid the cheers of the Central Empire officers.

Sparks flew from the cold steel as the blades clashed, with the

colonel slashing viciously to beat down Jimmy's guard.

The body of Colonel Goetz, their fallen hero, lay forgotten in the street.

When they had gotten well away from the crowd, Tim Donovan blew out his breath in a long sigh of relief. "Golly, Jimmy, that was close. That was certainly pulling the chestnuts out of the fire!"

Jimmy Christopher was looking grimly ahead. His thoughts were still on Colonel Goetz who lay dead in the snow. Men lived and were important, and were looked up to by their fellows. Then death struck, and they became nothing but inert clay. All their skill and all their importance, all their prestige and position became as nothing.

Operator 5 wondered if all this effort and risk was really worthwhile after all. What difference would it make, when they were all dead, whether the Central Empire conquered America? What difference did it make to the citizens of Carthage when Rome swept across her land in imperial triumph? The Carthaginians were dead for thousands of years and they lay under the ground, eaten by the same worms, decomposed by the same elements which turned to dust the bones of their Roman conquerors.

Death made no distinction between right and wrong, between victor and vanquished, between the brave and the cowardly. Suddenly Jimmy Christopher felt a great weariness. He had just fought a duel, and killed his man. Suppose he had been killed instead? He would be at peace now, without the great responsibility of carrying through this adventure which he had undertaken. Would he care now whether the troops of the Purple

Empire pushed the Americans into the Pacific Ocean or not? Would it matter to him that millions of Americans were living in virtual slavery throughout the land?

Suddenly he stiffened, and his lips tightened into a thin line. He must not let himself go along this road of defeatist philosophy.

Perhaps it would not matter of him personally what happened to the United States; but it would matter to all those youngsters who were growing up on the other side of the Rockies, and to all those unborn who would be forced to live under the alien yoke of oppression if the Central Empire conquered. If the Minute Men of 1776 had felt that way, there would never have teen any United States of America, any sovereign republic of the west. Those men had fought and suffered and died so that their descendants might live in freedom and not in slavery. And it was up to the Americans of today to suffer and die again so that *their* descendants might continue to live in liberty and not in slavery....

TIM DONOVAN knew exactly where he had to go. He drove the motor lorry up to Eleventh Street, then across Grant Park, around the Columbus Memorial and the Pasteur Monument, and into the long driveway that led out past the Shedd Aquarium toward the Adler Planetarium.

The Planetarium, sitting with its convex roof on the little promontory of land which jutted out into Lake Michigan, was virtually deserted at this hour of the day. Its rounded roof top was caked with snow, and there was a fresh layer of snow on the road, indicating that no vehicles had passed here for some time.

But along the footpath there were the prints of two pairs of feet.

Tim Donovan braked to a halt directly in front of the Planetarium. Jimmy Christopher reached down from the truck, threw a quick glance to right and left to make sure they were not observed, and walked swiftly around the building. Two American civilians emerged from the side of the building, and advanced to meet him. They appeared to be uncertain of how to act, until Jimmy said: "What did the stars say last night?"

Both these civilians were young men in their middle twenties. One of them answered him promptly: "The stars said we would meet a friend here today." They eyed his Central Empire uniform apprehensively, and threw questioning glances at the three motor lorries parked in front of the building.

Jimmy Christopher chuckled. "You needn't worry. I'm the friend you were to meet."

The two civilians stepped forward impulsively. "You are—"

"Operator 5," Jimmy finished for them. "What are your names?"

"I," said one of them, "am John Anderson. This is Leonard Buck."

Jimmy nodded. "I see you got our message from Minneapolis."

John Anderson asked him quickly: "They said you were moving from town to town, arranging for a simultaneous uprising. Is that true?"

"It's true. How many men could you muster here in Chicago?"

Anderson grinned. "There are two million men serving under Forced Labor Draft here in the city. If we could only get them enough guns, we could make out pretty well."

Jimmy nodded. "I'm going to leave three of my men here with you. They have instructions to make contact with one of our gun-running units from Sault Ste. Marie, across the Canadian border. They have a supply of rifles and ammunition—not enough by a long sight. But they'll give your men something to fight with. The men I leave will know how to arrange for boats to bring the stuff across. It's up to you to drill your recruits in secret and have them ready for the signal.

"Beginning this Sunday, you will keep a continuous watch posted right here on the lake front. When we are ready, the signal for a simultaneous uprising in twenty-four cities will be given. That signal will be three rockets. The men whom I leave will have rockets also, and when they see the signal, they will send up their rockets in turn as a signal to other units within sight."

Anderson asked anxiously: "You think we can succeed in such an uprising, Operator 5? The Central Empire has come down on us like a ton of brick. They could throw enough troops into this sector to crush any kind of uprising—"

"I know it," Jimmy Christopher said shortly. "I am not hoping that these risings will be successful. But I must have them take place, as a cover for what I expect to accomplish in Pittsburgh. Many of you will probably die here as a result of the uprising, as will thousands of men in the twenty-four other cities. But it is a necessary sacrifice. I must so arrange it that the Purple troops will be drawn away from the Pittsburgh area. It is my intention to seize that entire area and hold it, thus preventing the Purple Empire from completing their manufacture of the new Big Berthas."

Anderson said thoughtfully: "So you're asking us to commit suicide in order to insure the success of your operations?"

"That's what I'm asking," Jimmy Christopher said somberly. "If you are unwilling—?"

Anderson laughed bitterly. "Unwilling? We've been hoping for a chance like this. You can count on us, Operator 5!"

CHAPTER 5
RESCUE

ON SATURDAY evening—Coronation Eve—there was an artificial air of gala festivity in New York City. Central Empire officers paraded the streets in gorgeous dress uniforms donned especially for the occasion. By a special order of His Imperial Majesty, Rudolph I, all American civilians had been excused from labor for the evening, as well as for the following day, upon which the ceremony of the Emperor's coronation was to take place. But that surcease from work did not mean that they were to be permitted to rest peacefully at home. Instead, they were herded out by the thousands, to line the streets in solid throngs.

Many of these unfortunates were reminded of the good old days of American independence, when they had turned out to celebrate the fourth of July. In those days they had come voluntarily, full of joy and happiness, prepared to celebrate a great date in American history. Now, by imperial ukase, they were compelled to assume the semblance of gaiety in order to celebrate the triumph of the man who had reduced them to virtual serfdom.

Cordons of Central Empire troopers with rifles fixed in their bayonets stood guard along Broadway. Although many of the buildings in the theatrical district had been destroyed by the original bombardment of the Central Empire when New York had been captured, the Great White Way still remained a center of attraction. Many of the theaters had been rebuilt, and the American actors had been forced to continue with the presentation of their plays for the delectation of the Central Empire officers and their families.

Now, as a special sign of the good nature of Emperor Rudolph, booths had been erected all along Broadway, at which beer was dispensed to the American civilians. But each civilian, upon having his glass filled at the booth, was compelled to raise his hand in salute to the picture of Emperor Rudolph which was prominently displayed above the booth. Men, women and children were herded into line before the canteen, and anyone refusing to drink a toast of beer to the Purple Emperor would have been shot out of hand.

Many of these Americans would have preferred a good old-fashioned ice cream soda, without the toast to the Emperor. Had they been alone, they might have risked a swift bayonet thrust in the stomach; but the Purple Conquerors had shrewdly brought out the women and children as well. And since the men knew that their families would die with them at the first sign of disaffection, they swallowed their pride and drank the toast required of them. Never had such a hollow mockery of joyous gaiety been enacted in an American city.

While this forced celebration was going on, the Emperor Rudolph was holding court in the great, sumptuous palace which he had erected on the heights of Fort Tryon Park in the upper reaches of Manhattan, overlooking the Hudson River.*

In the Emperor's private suite on the second floor, Rudolph sat on a small dais, garbed in an informal ermine robe. At his side stood his suave, soft-spoken minister, Baron Julian Flexner. FLEXNER WAS saying: "If you please, Your Imperial

---

* AUTHOR'S NOTE: It will be recalled that this sumptuous palace overlooking the Hudson was the crowning act of ruthlessness of Emperor Rudolph. Four months before he had conscripted three thousand able-bodied Americans for the labor of building this palace. At its completion Rudolph had smirked and said that such a brilliant piece of architectural construction should be dedicated properly. "It is fitting," Rudolph had said, "that the hands which helped to build this palace for the Emperor of the World should never again build a lesser thing." And those three thousand Americans, at his order, had been driven over the side of a cliff at the point of the Central Empire troopers' bayonets, to be mashed to a pulp two hundred and thirty feet below, the rocks overhanging the Hudson. Thus had the imperial palace been fittingly dedicated in the eyes of Emperor Rudolph. And the widows and orphans of those three thousand Americans were still looking forward to the day when their husbands and fathers would be avenged.

Majesty, I have an interesting bit of news for you. Two persons were captured a few days ago in the city. Lieutenant Siegfried, of the Espionage Department, observed them acting in a suspicious manner on Fifth Avenue. He placed them in custody, and discovered by accident that one of the two was a woman. He turned them over to the Commandant of the Occupied Territory, but they refused to divulge their identity. This afternoon I was informed of the arrest, and went down to see the two people. Who do you think they are, sire?"

Rudolph was impatient. His thin, bloodless face was a mask of autocratic cruelty. "I am in no mood for riddles, Flexner. Speak quickly. Tell me your story."

"Yes, sire. Those two people are Sergeant MacTavish, of whom you have heard, and—a young woman!"

A glint of interest flickered in Rudolph's eyes. "A young woman? Who?"

Flexner spoke with smirking satisfaction. "A young woman, sire, whom I recognized at once. She is Nan Christopher, sire—the twin sister of Operator 5!"

Rudolph's eyes became pin-points of savage hatred. "Flexner! You are sure of this?"

"Positive, sire. See for yourself. I had them brought here, knowing that you would want to see them. They are waiting outside. Shall I summon them?"

"Quickly, Flexner, quickly. This is indeed good news. Operator 5 has flaunted me, defied me, and made fools of my men. To have his twin sister thrown into my hands like this is almost incredible!"

Flexner bowed, went swiftly to the door, and spoke to the guard in the corridor. In a moment Nan and MacTavish were led in, handcuffed, accompanied by a guard of four troopers. MacTavish was disheveled. His tie hung crooked, and the left sleeve of his coat was ripped. There was a wide, open gash in the side of his cheek. But one of the troopers who held him also gave evidence of having suffered rough treatment. The man's eye was blackened, and there was a wide strip of adhesive across his nose. It was very apparent that MacTavish had put up a battle.

Nan Christopher looked even smaller than she was, alongside the huge Canadian sergeant. Her hat was gone, and she looked really boyish in the close haircut that she had given herself for this expedition. She had deliberately sacrificed her beautiful, soft hair for the purpose of disguising herself as a man. Her clothes were still ripped down the front where Lieutenant Siegfried had torn them; and she was holding the ends together in order to prevent her small white breasts from being exposed to view. Both she and MacTavish exhibited no sign of fear or awe as they were led up to the dais upon which Rudolph sat.

The Emperor was almost in a genial mood now. He murmured: "Excellent, Flexner. It is she, without a doubt. I can see the resemblance at once. It is Operator 5's sister."

Flexner smiled. "I trust Your Majesty is satisfied."

"Yes, indeed, Flexner. Yes, indeed." The Emperor leaned forward in his throne-like chair, and addressed the prisoners. "Perhaps you will be good enough to tell me," he said silkily, "what you were doing here in New York?"

Nan Christopher met his gaze with defiance. Then she

suddenly smiled saucily. "Your Majesty, we were worried about the poor squirrels in Central Park. Your brave troops certainly have no time to feed the poor squirrels, so the sergeant and I came to New York to see that the squirrels are fed."

Rudolph's forehead furrowed in anger. He snarled: "You will be very glad to talk when I get through with you, young woman!"

MacTavish grew red in the face and took an impulsive step forward, but he was stopped by the bayonet of one of the guards, pressing against his stomach.

"Take them away!" Rudolph barked. "After my coronation tomorrow, we will attend to them!"

AS THEY were about to be led out, Flexner exclaimed: "Wait, sire." He bent and whispered in Rudolph's ear.

Rudolph's face lit up with a wicked light. "Excellent, excellent." He raised a hand to the troopers. "Bring them back here!"

Nan and MacTavish were led back to the dais.

Rudolph was smiling twistedly. "Baron Flexner has made a very good suggestion. Instead of waiting until after my coronation, we shall have some diversion with you two, at once. We will erect a gibbet in front of St. Patrick's Cathedral. Tomorrow morning you, Miss Christopher, will be suspended by your feet from that gibbet. People have been known to live for a long time in that position. You will have an excellent upside-down view of the coronation ceremonies. Ha, ha, I think Flexner is very clever, do you not?"

MacTavish's big manacled hand clenched in sudden fury. "Damn you," he shouted, "you can't do that—"

Rudolph raised his eyebrows. "No? Perhaps you would like

to spare the young lady the torture of being hung upside down. In that case, all you need to do is to inform me what you were doing here. Baron Flexner suggests that you came to New York to foment a rebellion. Whom did you meet here? Who are your accomplices? Give us their names, and Miss Christopher will be spared."

MacTavish hesitated, and Nan exclaimed: "No, no, Mac. For God's sake, be silent!"

MacTavish gulped. "Go to hell, Your Majesty!" he exclaimed.

Rudolph snarled: "Tomorrow, when Miss Christopher is suspended by her feet, you, my brave sergeant, will be crucified—also upside down!"

He waved to Flexner. "Now—take them to St. Patrick's Cathedral at once. Have them in readiness for the ceremonies tomorrow!"

Flexner bowed low. "I will attend to everything, sire."

He backed out of the room, and the troopers led Nan and MacTavish after him.

Outside, Flexner ordered a staff car brought around, and Nan and the sergeant were hustled into it, with four troopers sitting on guard. The troopers had removed the bayonets from their rifles, and were holding the sharp points of the steel against their sides. Flexner moved into the front seat beside the driver, and ordered: "To St. Patrick's Cathedral!"

The driver saluted, and sent the car lolling down the steep road from Fort Tryon Park. He swung into Riverside Drive, and proceeded down along the shore of the Hudson. In the river, Nan and MacTavish could see the lights of the great Central

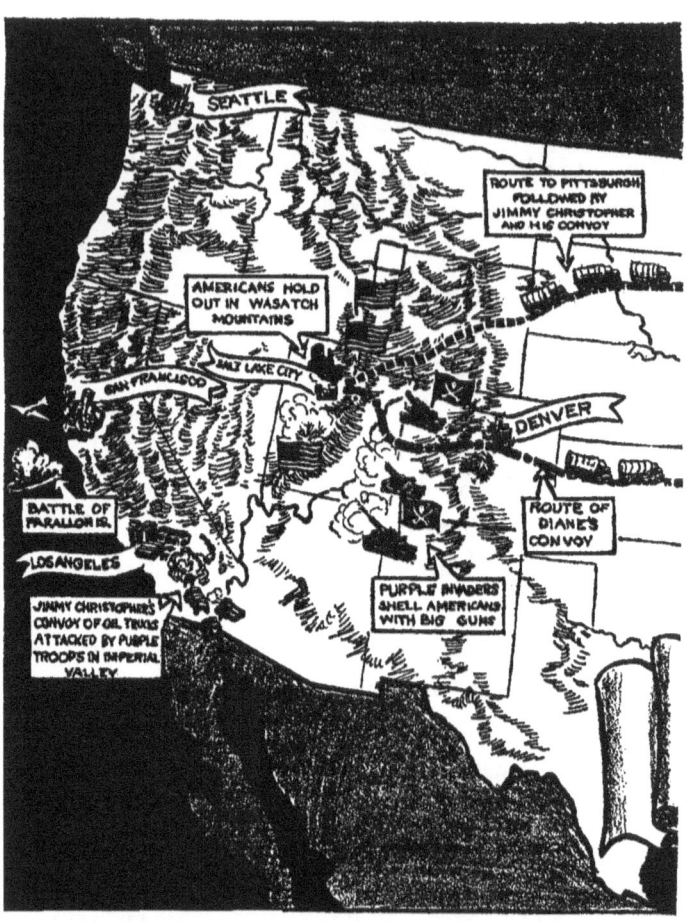

Empire battleships anchored there. Numerous planes were circling in the air above them, dropping illuminated fireworks, preparing for the celebration tomorrow.

Flexner turned around in his seat and grinned at them evilly.

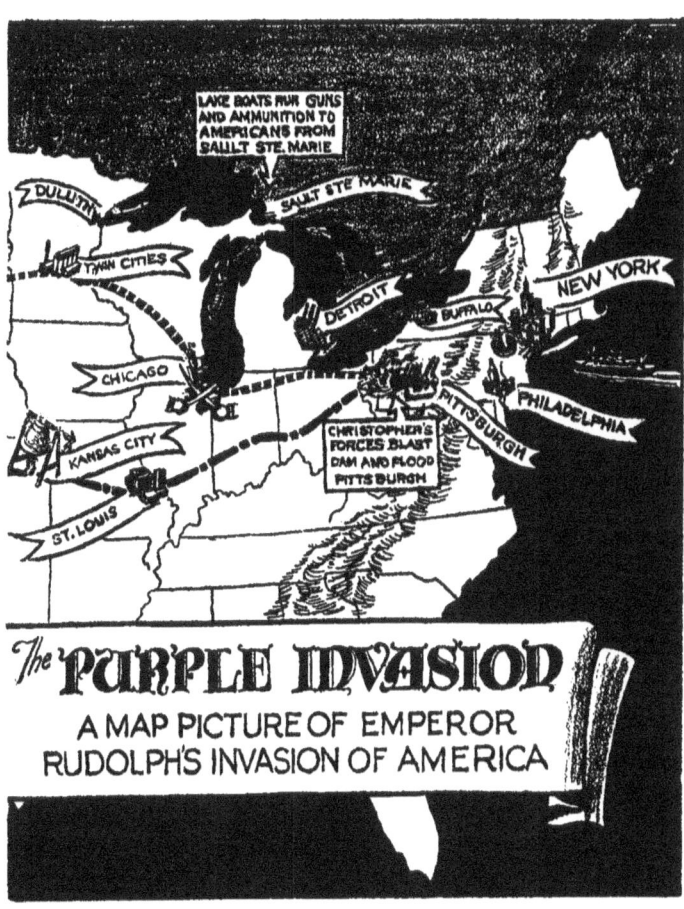

"You should be highly honored at being made such an important part of the coronation ceremony. You—"

He never finished the sentence.

Suddenly the dark roadway became alive with shadowy figures. Dozens of men swarmed in the path of the speeding automobile, springing across the road, and waving their hands. The driver of the staff car began to apply his brakes in puzzlement. As the car slowed up, the headlights illuminated the faces of those men in the road, and MacTavish exclaimed under his breath: "Lacord! There's Mayor Lacord!"

Baron Flexner shouted to the driver excitedly: "Go on, you fool! Drive through them. It's the Americans. They're trying to effect a rescue—"

The driver swore lustily, and started to put his foot down on the gas. MacTavish twisted sideways, away from the point of the bayonet which his guard was holding against him, and brought his elbow up in a smashing crack to the jaw of the guard. The man crumpled. MacTavish leaned swiftly forward, raised his manacled hands, and brought them down hard upon the skull of the driver. The Central Empire driver slumped at the wheel.

Flexner reached frantically for his gun.

But it was too late. The Americans had wrenched open the doors of the car, and were now swarming all around it. In a moment Flexner had been overpowered, as had the other guard in the rear.

Lacord's perspiring face appeared. The Mayor exclaimed: "Glory be to God! We heard by the underground grapevine that you two had been taken from the jail to Rudolph's headquarters. We were waiting here, hoping to stop you on the way back. And we succeeded!"

MacTavish pressed Lacord's hand. "Good man!" he exclaimed. "That was smart thinking." Flexner was silent in the grip of two of the Americans. Nan's eyes were wet with happy tears.

68

In a moment Flexner and the other Central Empire soldiers had been bundled out of the car and were carried away into the darkness by the Americans. Lacord and two others remained. One of the Americans took the wheel of the car, and they all piled in. The driver swung the car in a wide circle, and headed north again.

"Where are we going?" MacTavish asked.

"We'll cut east, then swing down toward the Polo Grounds. Most of my men are waiting for us there. Have you heard the news yet?"

"What news?" Nan breathed.

"About your brother, Miss Christopher," Lacord said. "He's in Pittsburgh. A couple of his men arrived this morning. We're to be ready for a signal, to start an uprising here. He made his way across the country with three motor lorries, and dropped men off at all the key cities. Miss Diane Elliot took three more lorries and is covering the southern part of the United States, arranging for simultaneous rebellions all over the country. At a given signal there will be some twenty uprisings. Operator 5 figures that these uprisings will draw the Central Empire troops from the neighborhood of Pittsburgh, and he'll have an opportunity to capture the steel mills. What he's going to do after he captures them, God only knows. But it's a bold stroke—risky!"

Nan was smiling happily.

"He'll succeed—in whatever he undertakes. And I'm sure he knows what he's doing!"

"God grant that he does," Lacord said fervently. "Because we're risking our lives and the lives of our families at his order!"

CHAPTER 6
THE CONVOYS COME
THROUGH

THREE MOTOR lorries rumbled to a stop on the high-road alongside the abandoned airport at Freedom, Pennsylvania, some five miles northwest of the Allegheny County line, and about fifteen miles from the city of Pittsburgh. This was on the highway from Newcastle, and the going was rough, because the road was rutted and scarred by the shell-fire which the Purple Empire had laid down in its original advance through Pennsylvania. As a result, this road was not being used by the Central Empire troops, and the lorries had come through without being stopped for questioning.

Snow lay thick on the airport field and in the ditch along the road as Tim Donovan and Operator 5 descended from the cab of the first truck. Half a dozen men climbed out of the other two trucks. Others had been left along the way, dropped off by twos and threes all along the route, stationed in towns where they would organize rebellion.

Now, the half dozen remaining Americans ran up and down briskly, swinging their hands to keep the cold from permeating through their bodies. Raw, wintry blasts of wind swept across the airport, cutting at their faces with the keenness of newly sharpened blades. Tim Donovan still wore the bandage on his face, and he grinned stiffly in the cold at Operator 5.

"Gee, Jimmy, I hope those guys are on time. If we have to wait here very long, we'll be frozen stiff!"

Almost as he finished speaking, dark figures began to emerge from the doorway of the Operations Building at the far end of the field. Snow crunched under the feet of a hundred men who came out of that building and approached the truck.

These men were Americans, but they were all garbed in the uniform of Central Empire troopers. One man's uniform tunic carried the epaulets of a captain of artillery. This one approached the truck, and when his eyes lighted on Jimmy Christopher, he smiled broadly, advanced with outstretched hand.

Jimmy shook hands with him. "Good work, Ames. I see you equipped all your men with uniforms and rifles."

Ames grinned. "We've broken into the Quartermaster's supply room, and stole these uniforms and weapons. We have a hundred rifles, ten machine guns, and six dozen of those new flame grenades that the Central Empire have begun to use. We got your message on the amateur radio hook-up, and we made sure to be here on time."

Jimmy Christopher said to his own men: "Boys, I want you to meet Frank Ames, who's been in charge of American Intelligence in Pennsylvania since the beginning of the Central Empire invasion. He's going to cooperate with us tonight."

Ames shook hands with Jimmy's men, then asked: "What is your plan, Operator 5?"

"I want to do two things," Jimmy Christopher told him. "First, I want to rescue Franklin Ransom, who is being held somewhere here in Pittsburgh. Second, I want to take possession of the Pittsburgh area. I want to destroy every one of the steel mills, and the mines. I want to make it impossible for the Central Empire to manufacture any more guns."

Ames hesitated. "I've carried out all the instructions that you gave on the radio, Operator 5. I got uniforms for these men, and I've smuggled five hundred other men into Pittsburgh in the last three days. They're hiding in the ruined buildings and in the sewers, ready to come out when you give the signal. But I can't see how we can possibly succeed. Even if we should surprise the Central Empire guard in the city, there are enough troops within a twenty-mile radius to swamp us—"

"I've taken care of that," Jimmy Christopher said. "We've arranged for uprisings in twenty-four cities all over the country. They are all going to occur simultaneously, and the Purple troops will have to be rushed out in all directions to take care of these rebellions. I figure that they'll leave only a skeleton guard here in Pennsylvania, because everything will be quiet in this state. That should give us an opportunity to do our job."

Ames' eyes lighted up with sudden enthusiasm. "That's swell, Operator 5. I begin to think we have a chance. When do we start?"

"As soon as Miss Elliot arrives. She has three more trucks, and she's working her way across to meet us here, working through Evansville, Cincinnati, Dayton and Columbus." Jimmy frowned. He glanced at his watch. "She should have been here before—"

He was stopped by a sudden joyful exclamation from Tim Donovan, "There they are!" the lad exclaimed, pointing down the road.

SURE ENOUGH, three more motor lorries became visible in the night, bumping across the shell-scarred road. In a few moments the lorries pulled up alongside the airport, and Diane Elliot, accompanied by another half dozen men, reached down from the truck. Diane was dressed in the uniform of a staff captain, but she had not cut her hair. It was bunched up under her uniform cap, and her greatcoat hid the soft feminine contours of her body. Her eyes were sparkling with eagerness as she swiftly kissed Operator 5 and hugged Tim Donovan.

It did not take her long to report. "I've arranged everything, Jimmy," she said enthusiastically. "I dropped men off in eleven cities, and made all arrangements for the rebellion to take place. Three rockets will be the signal."

Jimmy Christopher nodded. He turned to Ames. "That's Pittsburgh over there, isn't it?" he asked, pointing across the open country toward a mass of fiery light and flame which glowed from the craggy ground upon which the city of Pittsburgh was built, and which was plainly visible from the airport They could clearly see the dense mass of factories, mills and warehouses, with spouting locomotives moving along the tracks which grid ironed the city, the whole thing overhung with smoke and mist.

"That's Pittsburgh," Ames said. "Over there, to your right, you can see Mount Washington, where the Central Empire engineers have moved the Big Berthas which they've already constructed. There are five of them, and they expect to put them into operation within a few days."

Jimmy Christopher's eyes narrowed. "Mount Washington, eh," he repeated thoughtfully. "How well is it fortified?"

"They've got concrete dug-outs up there, and half a dozen

big emplacements for the huge Big Berthas. They've also got a concrete cellar that's proof against airplane bombs. The Big Berthas are placed under big concrete arches which are also supposed to be impregnable, against any kind of aerial bombs. They've moved up a supply of food and water, too, but they haven't yet assigned a full garrison to it. I guess they don't think it's necessary, right here in the heart of their army. Once the Big Berthas begin operating, though, I guess they'll throw a half a regiment up on that hill."

Jimmy Christopher was suddenly smiling. "That's our objective, Ames!" he said softly. "We'll take Mount Washington. It'll give us the Big Berthas, and we'll be able to destroy every factory in the Pittsburgh district from that vantage point. Then let them come and take us!"

Ames and his men, who had crowded around the small group, stared at Operator 5 open-mouthed. There was a moment of stunned silence among them as they slowly realized the enormous daring of Jimmy Christopher's plan. Then a low cheer suddenly went up from among them.

Ames exclaimed: "We'll do it, Operator 5! There's nothing to lose, and everything to gain. But my God, we can't destroy the factories. There must be fifty thousand men in those shops, and they're all shackled there, unable to leave. They'd all perish."

"Maybe we can free them," Jimmy Christopher said grimly. "We've got to free Franklin Ransom, so perhaps we can do the job complete. Let's go. Leave two men here, with rockets. We've stationed men at ten-mile intervals all the way across the country. When they see your rockets they'll send off their own, and the rockets going up all the way across the country will give the signal for the rebellion."

"How are we to know when to send the rockets up?" one of the men asked.

Jimmy Christopher looked across toward Pittsburgh, where Mount Washington was plainly visible. "We'll signal you from there," he said, "with a torch. When you see a torch flaring from there, send up your rockets."

Ames said eagerly: "There's an old church there at the top of Mount Washington. It survived the bombardment. You can't see it now, because it's dark. But there's a tall steeple on it, and if you wave the torch from there, it could be easily seen from here."

JIMMY NODDED. "We'll do it that way. Ames, you and your men pile into the lorries. When we reach Pittsburgh, you'll scatter, and round up all the women and children of the families of our Americans who are shackled in the factories. Tell them to make for Mount Washington. Once we get them out of the hands of the Central Empire, our Americans won't be worried about reprisal. I'll take twenty men and march toward the factory where Ransom is being held prisoner. Give me a half dozen of those name bombs. I think we'll be able to use them."

Ames saluted, and ordered his men to get into the trucks. Jimmy Christopher shook hands with him, said: "Look here, Frank, I'm going to plan my campaign on the basis of the information you've given me. I hope it's reliable. If it isn't, thousands of Americans will die tonight—for nothing."

"You can trust me, sir," Ames said quietly. "Everything I've told you about Mount Washington is correct. And now that you've advanced this idea, I can see that it would be the ideal place to hold against the enemy. With the Big Berthas, and the ammunition that's stored up there, and the food and water, we could hold it against an army for a long time." His face flushed with enthusiasm. "Operator 5, the more I think of it, the better I like it! It's a brilliant idea. It'll tie up all the Central Empire's plans for turning the Big Berthas on our own troops; it'll even enable us to bombard the Purple armies, and take them in the rear."

"Let's hope it turns out that way," Jimmy Christopher said quietly. "This means more to us than you can imagine, Ames. At Toledo, we received a message through the amateur radio, from Z-7. He informs us that the enemy is pressing them hard all along the line, and they won't be able to hold their positions in the Wasatch Mountains for more than a few days longer. Once the Purple troops get through the Wasatch Range, there'll be no stopping them this side of the Sierra Nevadas—and that means that they'll be within range of the West Coast cities. They'll make a shambles of every city and town in Washington, Oregon and California with their big guns."

Ames' eyes widened, as he looked from Tim Donovan to Diane Elliot, then back at Jimmy Christopher. "No! I hadn't imagined it was as serious as that. It means that we've got to succeed here, that we've got to create enough diversion here to stop the Purple troops from advancing in the West—"

"We've got to do more than create a diversion," Jimmy said grimly. "We've got to destroy every source of the enemy's munitions supplies, and cripple the Central Empire at this point. The life of America depends on it!"

Ames said tightly: "You can count on us, every man of us, Operator 5!" He swung around, singled out twenty men whom he ordered to join Jimmy, Diane and Tim in the leading truck.

"You'd better let one of those twenty men drive the truck," he told Jimmy. "He knows just where to go."

Operator 5 nodded, motioned to Tim and Diane to get into the lorry. He followed them in, with the twenty men whom Ames had assigned to them, and in a moment the truck pulled away, leaving the others to follow.

Diane put a cold hand on Operator 5's arm. "Jimmy!" she said softly. "Have we really got a chance of succeeding at this?"

"You want the truth, Di?" Jimmy said. "Well, we have about one chance in five thousand of succeeding. But we've got to do it, Di. It's a crazy, wild, impractical, hopeless scheme. But it's the only thing left for us to do. Perhaps none of us here will survive this night. Perhaps thousands of other Americans in the other twenty-four cities will die in the abortive rebellions. But if we perish, we have the satisfaction of knowing that we've tried—and tried hard."

Diane and Jimmy were silent for a moment, and then they heard Tim Donovan in the darkness of the truck beside them, moving about.

"What are you doing, Tim?" Jimmy asked.

"I'm taking this damned bandage off my head," Tim Donovan told him. "If there's going to be any real action tonight, I want to be able to see it without blinkers!"

CHAPTER 7
WELCOME FOR VON
INNSBRUCK

THE LONG low Experimental Building of the Central Empire sat squatty in the fork formed by the Allegheny and Monongahela Rivers, in that portion of the city of Pittsburgh which had once been known as the Golden Triangle. Where once there had risen the tall towers of modern office buildings, where once had glittered the lights of theaters and gay streets, there was now spread out this vast, sprawling structure devoted to the discovery of new alloy for guns and of new chemicals for explosives and gases with which to destroy the American defenses.

Pittsburgh had put up a stiff defense against the advance of the Central Empire, and as a result the city had been virtually destroyed. Hardly a building had been left standing; and upon those smoldering ruins the Central Empire had built many new, vast structures for the production of steel.

Jimmy Christopher had been in Pittsburgh many times before, but there was nothing about the city which was recognizable now. It all seemed strange, grotesque, as he rode up to the door of the Experimental Building in the motor lorry. Ugly black buildings spread out in every direction, and between them there were no longer streets and sidewalks, but wide reaches of snow, with here and there a pit or a mound to show where the ground had been deeply scarred by the huge shells of the enemy bombardment, or where the heaped ruins of some destroyed building still lay where they had fallen—no doubt entombing the bodies of many Americans.

To the east there rose the funnels of hundreds of newly erected blast furnaces, from which streamers of intermittent flame belched forth as indication that captive Americans were working there constantly. The raucous clangor of heavy machinery sounded through the night with the persistent din of a thousand steel hammers. And from the building before which they had stopped, Jimmy and Diane and Tim could hear the shouts of men and sizzling of molten iron being poured from open hearth furnaces.

The driver of the motor lorry, an American named Ericson, spoke over his shoulder to Jimmy: "This is the Experimental Building, Operator 5. This is where they've got Franklin Ransom. What do we do—go in and take him out?"

The twenty men crowded into the truck with Jimmy were eager, tense, ready for the adventure. But Jimmy Christopher shook his head.

"Not yet, Ericson," he said. "We've got to be sure of every step. I'm going in first, and look over the lay of the land. I want to find out just where Ransom is being kept, and just how much time we need to release all these other men before we destroy the factory. I'm going in. The rest of you wait out here for me."

The men all maintained absolute silence as Jimmy Christopher descended from the lorry and approached the Corporal of the Guard who stood at the entrance of the building.

The Corporal saluted stiffly at face of the swanky young major who approached him. Jimmy said: "Take me to your commandant at once. Imperial business."

The man complied at once. There was no question in his mind but that everything was as it should be. He had seen the Central Empire motor lorry pull up at the door, with the insignia of the Purple Emperor painted upon the side of the hood. He had seen the men in Central Empire uniforms within that lorry, and he had seen the authoritative looking young major descend from the truck. Everything appeared to be in order, and the corporal said respectfully: "This way, sir. Colonel Goermann is in his office at the moment. Will you be good enough to follow me?"

The clanging sounds of activity in the experimental shops grew louder as Jimmy followed his guide into the office of the Commandant.

COLONEL GOERMANN'S round, bald head bobbed up from the newspaper which he was reading at his desk. He frowned, put down the paper, and arose, looking inquiringly at Jimmy Christopher.

Jimmy clicked his heels together, stood smartly at attention, and saluted. "Major von Innsbruck," he said crisply, "reporting to Colonel Goermann upon imperial business."

Operator 5 was taut, watching the commandant closely as he announced himself. Goermann, he had heard, was nobody's fool. It would be a difficult job to pull the wool over his eyes; yet it had to be tried if the daring plan was to succeed. Everything depended upon how Goermann reacted in the first moments of the interview.

The Colonel's reaction to Jimmy Christopher's announcement of his name and rank was more or less startling. His thin lips broke into a wide smile of welcome.

"Von Innsbruck!" he exclaimed. "You are welcome indeed, Major. I have been hearing about you, and I was wondering if I should ever have the pleasure of meeting you personally!"

The Colonel came around the desk quickly, and extended a hand. "Permit me, Major, to shake hands with you. It is not often that one has the pleasure of meeting so distinguished a member of His Imperial Majesty's forces!"

Jimmy's eyes narrowed suspiciously as he accepted the Colonel's proffered hand. This was hardly what he had expected. He had really anticipated surliness and suspicion. Instead, he was welcomed with unexpected warmth.

"You know me, my Colonel?" Jimmy asked cautiously. "You say—you have heard of me?"

"But yes, my dear Major von Innsbruck. Who has not heard of you? Here—" he reached over to the desk and snatched up the newspaper which he was reading—"see for yourself!"

He thrust the newspaper into Jimmy's hand. Jimmy Christopher's eyes widened as he glanced across the page. This paper was *The Central Empire Daily News*. It was the official newspaper of the Purple Empire, and it had grown to enjoy a wide circulation. Not only did the officers and men of the Central Empire purchase it, but civilians in every city and town in the country were compelled to buy it likewise. It did not matter that they could not read the unfamiliar characters of the language of the Central Empire: they had to buy the paper anyway, or incur the severe displeasure of the commandant of their occupied territory.

Now, Jimmy Christopher read the four-column headline, and he suddenly understood why Colonel Goermann was so glad to see him. This is what he read:

NOTED SWORDSMAN MEETS HIS MATCH

On Thursday morning, Colonel Herman Goetz, the victor of forty-two duels, finally met his match in the person of a hitherto unknown young major by the name of von Innsbruck. Interviewed by a reporter of the *Central Empire Daily News*, Brigadier General von Zuppert stated that never in his life had he been privileged to witness so brilliant an exhibition of swordsmanship. It is his firm conviction that Major von Innsbruck is without a peer in his mastery of the foils. The General hopes to meet von Innsbruck in New York on Sunday for the coronation ceremonies, and he intends to stage several exhibition fencing matches in order to convince the world of von Innsbruck's skill....

Goermann was talking excitedly, telling Jimmy that he had always disliked Colonel Goetz, had always entertained a secret hope that Goetz would eventually meet his match with the sabre.

BUT JIMMY was only appearing to listen. In reality, his eyes were scanning the other news items. Apparently the paper had just come out, and there was information of vital interest in a story in the first column and another story in a box at the top of the page. The box contained the following item:

CAPTURE OF TWO DANGEROUS ENEMIES OF THE EMPIRE

It is quite true that the Americans in the conquered territory are constantly plotting rebellion against our Imperial Rudolph. Only today, Baron Julian Flexner recognized, among prisoners at the Occupied Territory Headquarters, two persons who are closely associated with the arch enemy of the Central Empire— the man who is known as Operator 5.

Those two persons were Sergeant Aloysius MacTavish, and Operator 5's twin sister, Nan Christopher. They had been arrested here while in disguise by our keen-eyed Lieutenant Siegfried of the Espionage Service. It has been proved that they were in New York to plot an uprising. While being taken from the Emperor's palace back to the jail, a number of Americans ambushed their car and carried them off, together with Baron Flexner. But out valiant troops succeeded in recapturing them just as they were holding a meeting in the ruins of their Polo Grounds. Baron Flexner was rescued.

Nan Christopher and Sergeant MacTavish will be exhibited tomorrow at the coronation ceremonies upon a special gibbet which is being erected opposite St. Patrick's Cathedral. Nan Christopher will be suspended by her feet, while Sergeant MacTavish will be crucified. All true subjects of the Central Empire will delight to hear that these two are to be accorded the punishment they deserve.

At the time of their capture they were organizing some two hundred Americans among the ruins of the Polo Grounds, with a view to attacking St. Patrick's Cathedral tomorrow during the ceremonies. The Americans under their former Mayor, Lacord, put up a stiff resistance, but our machine guns mowed them down. Some twenty-five or thirty were captured together with MacTavish and the Christopher woman, and those twenty-five will be hung tomorrow as an example to others....

Jimmy Christopher's eyes were bleak as he read this item. He had counted much on the presence of Nan and MacTavish in New York, hoping that they would be able to direct a powerful uprising at the time when the signal was given. Now, not only was the rebellion in New York crushed before it had begun, but Nan and MacTavish were in grave danger.

While Goermann continued to praise him to the skies volubly, a gray coldness gripped at Jimmy Christopher's heart. Nan and MacTavish had failed. No doubt they had tried, and tried hard. But luck had been against them. His own sister was to be sacrificed at the coronation ceremony tomorrow, and there was nothing—absolutely nothing in the world—that he could do about it. He must let Nan and MacTavish perish there in New York, and go on with his work here.

Goermann was looking at him queerly now. "You are not listening, Major von Innsbruck. There is something that interests you in the paper?"

Jimmy snapped out of it. "Yes, yes, my Colonel, it is this item which interests me." He pointed to the story in the first column which told how a great convoy of supply ships was sailing from

Europe, with new guns and ammunition manufactured in the Skoda, Vickers & Krupp plants in Czechoslovakia, England and Germany. Two hundred of the giant Skoda howitzers were part of that tremendous shipment, which was expected to arrive in New York within a short time. The news story went on to relate that once these guns and munitions were in the hands of the Central Empire troops, they would be able to press south into Mexico and thence farther on to conquer both continents of America.

"That is very good news," Jimmy said. "It will mean the spread of the Purple Empire to every part of the world."

Goermann nodded. "True, Major von Innsbruck. The star of the Central Empire is in the ascendant. But tell me, what is your mission here?"

Jimmy handed back the paper, trying not to think of Nan and MacTavish in New York. Resolutely he tore his mind from images of his sister about to be executed. Nothing of his feeling showed in his face as he said to Goermann: "I am proceeding to New York for the coronation. I have been ordered to stop here and interview the American inventor, Franklin Ransom. The Emperor wishes a personal report on his progress."

"Gladly," Goermann said. "Come with me, please, and I will show him to you."

JIMMY FOLLOWED the Colonel through the immensely long building, passing shop after shop where the open hearths were being operated by shackled Americans. As he went through the rooms, his eyes darted here and there, estimating the possibilities of releasing all these men when the time came. At last they were brought into the room where Ransom and Daws still sat at their bench.

Both men seemed to be exhausted, and they were lying on the hard wooden benches, snatching a bit of sleep. They awoke with a start as the guards clanged their rifles and stood to attention.

Jimmy Christopher's heart went out to Franklin Ransom. The man was haggard, with a misery that spoke through his eyes. Jimmy had heard the story of Franklin Ransom, had heard how his two children were held as hostages to insure his successful completion of the test for ransomite three. He knew under what a strain Ransom must be working.

The scientist looked up dully as Goermann said: "My goot friendt, I wish you to meet Major von Innsbruck who has come to interview you at the request of the Emperor."

Young Henry Daws scowled at Jimmy and at Goermann, but Ransom said wearily: "I hope to be finished some time during the night, if that is what you wish to know. You may tell that to the Emperor. Ask him for God's sake to spare my two children."

Jimmy Christopher stepped close to the work-bench, leaned over it, and said in a low voice: "I will do my best for you, Mr. Ransom." He glanced sideways, saw that Goermann was not listening to them, but was idly inspecting a number of the blue-prints on the table. Jimmy lowered his voice even more, virtually whispered: "I am Operator 5!"

He watched out of the corner of his eye to see if Goermann had heard, but the Colonel had not caught the word. Ransom and Daws had heard what he said, both of them started perceptibly, then controlled themselves by a visible effort. Ransom looked up at Jimmy suspiciously, studying Operator 5's face.

Jimmy hurried on, under his breath: "We are going to try to rescue you within the next two or three hours. Be prepared to leave. Take your plans with you."

There was a sudden light of hope in Ransom's eye, but it quickly faded. "You—you couldn't get me out of here. My shackles—"

He stopped as Goermann put down the blueprints he had been studying and turned to hear what was being said.

Jimmy broke in hastily, speaking for the benefit of the Colonel: "Then I can tell his Imperial Majesty definitely, that ransomite three will be ready during the night?"

Ransom took the cue. "Yes, yes. It will be ready. You will do what you can about my children?"

"Have no fear for your children, Mr. Ransom," Jimmy said significantly. "They will be taken care of."

Goermann interrupted the conversation. "Of course, my goot friendt, your children will be unharmed. Indeed, I think that His Imperial Majesty will grant you a Medal of the Empire for your distinguished service in developing ransomite three."

Goermann's eyes were twinkling sardonically as he said this. "No doubt you will appreciate receiving such an award from the Central Empire. Ha, ha!"

He turned, frowning, as an orderly entered with a message. "Not now," he said gruffly. "Wait for me in the office. I will be there shortly."

Jimmy had snatched the opportunity while Goermann was

talking to the orderly, to whisper hurriedly to Ransom: "Be prepared. We'll be back tonight!"

That was all he had time for, and then Goermann had swung back to him. He thanked the Colonel for the interview, and they left Ransom and Daws. The two American captives watched them go through the arched doorway. What was in the mind of Ransom and Daws was hard to say at the moment. Was it suspicion? Was it hope? But whatever it was, there seemed to be a new alertness about them, a resurgence of hope in their eyes.

This might be some trap—it might be an officer of the Central Empire posing as Operator 5—but if that were so, they could not be worse off. Eagerly they whispered to each other, careful not to excite the suspicions of the guard.

"I don't need the plans," Ransom said. "I've got everything in my mind. The alloy is right, and I could have given it to Goermann this morning. I was holding out, hoping against hope that something would happen. And it seems that God listened to my prayers. Do you really think, Henry, that the man was Operator 5?"

Daws was thoughtful. "We'll know soon enough. But, Mr. Ransom—what about these shackles?"

Ransom shrugged. "Let us trust in God, Henry!"

Outside in Goermann's office again, Jimmy Christopher shook hands with the Colonel, and said: "I have some business to transact here in Pittsburgh, before I go on to New York. If I may, I shall drop in to see you later in the evening."

"Delighted," Goermann said. "I should like to have you give me a few pointers in the handling of the sabre."

"It will be a pleasure," Jimmy Christopher said smoothly. "I should like nothing better than to give you a few lessons with the sabre!"

Goermann saw him to the door, then returned and took the message which the orderly handed him.

"It is from the Telegraph Bureau, my Colonel," the orderly said. "The message is being sent to all commandants of occupied territory in the East."

Goermann nodded, and opened the message. It was from Imperial Espionage Headquarters in New York, and it read as follows:

TO ALL MILITARY COMMANDANTS:

MAN POSING AS MAJOR VON INNSBRUCK OF 19TH HUSSARS REPORTED TO HAVE KILLED COLONEL GOETZ IN DUEL... NO SUCH OFFI-CER APPEARS ON ROSTER OF 19TH IMPERIAL HUSSARS... IMPOSTOR PROBABLY AN AMERI-CAN SPY... APPARENTLY YOUNG BUT CARRIES HIMSELF WITH MUCH POISE... BLUE EYES... STRAIGHT NOSE... FIRM JAW AND MOUTH... IMPERIAL MUSTACHE... ALL COMMANDANTS OF OCCUPIED TERRITORIES ARE INSTRUCTED TO KEEP WATCH FOR THIS MAN AND APPRE-HEND HIM... HE WAS LAST SEEN TRAVELING TOWARD PITTSBURGH WITH THREE MOTOR LORRIES... SPEAKS OUR LANGUAGE LIKE NATIVE AND CARRIES HIMSELF EXACTLY LIKE CENTRAL

EMPIRE OFFICER… IS EXPERT SWORDSMAN…
IT IS POSSIBLE THIS MAN IS OPERATOR 5 IN
DISGUISE IF SO HIS CAPTOR WILL BE AMPLY
REWARDED.

Colonel Goermann stood for a moment, holding the message
in his hand, and staring out into the night after Jimmy Christopher's lorry had disappeared. Then a slow smile wreathed itself
about his thin lips.

"So, he will give me a lesson with the sabre, eh? He is coming
back to see me, no? I shall make sure," he said softly to himself,
"to prepare a very surprising welcome for this Major von Innsbruck!"

CHAPTER 8
ROCKETS FOR REVOLT

JIMMY CHRISTOPHER had mounted into the cab
beside Ericson, the driver of the lorry. Now Ericson, without having to wait for instructions, drove northwest across the
Liberty Avenue Bridge, which was the only bridge left standing
across the Allegheny River. Then he swung into the rutted roadway, covered with snow, of what had once been Château Street.

They passed a number of Frank Ames' Americans in the
Central Empire uniforms, who were escorting women and children through the streets. Jimmy Christopher nodded in silent
satisfaction. Acting under cover of their uniforms, Ames' men
were taking the wives and children of the American workers

down across the North Side Bridge over the Ohio and into the Mount Washington Park section.

There were so many of the Central Empire troopers moving about in the city that no one even thought to stop or question these men who were apparently moving American captives from one place of confinement to another. Such movements of captives were common in all the Central Empire cities, for it was a fixed principle of the conquerors not to give the American civilians any peace, nor to permit them to remain in one place too long. Rudolph understood the constant threat of rebellion, and it was his policy not to permit the Americans to get set in any one locality.

Ames and his men were doing their part. It was up to Jimmy to do his part.

From inside of the truck, Diane called out anxiously: "Was everything all right at the Experimental Building, Jimmy?"

"I don't know," Jimmy told her. "I didn't have much of a chance to talk to Ransom. I merely warned him that we'd be back in two or three hours. He started to tell me something about his shackles, about not being able to get away, but he couldn't finish, because Goermann was close to us." He shrugged. "We'll have to meet the obstacles as they arise tonight, Di."

Ericson continued north on Château Street, saying: "There's the new church, that was erected just before the Central Empire Invasion started. You can go up in the belfry, and give the signal to the men at the airport. They'll surely see your torch from there."

They were driving up close to the bank of the Ohio River

at this point, and Jimmy Christopher pointed out across at Brunot's Island, sitting in the middle of the river. Across the island there arose the huge concrete mass of a gravity dam, spanning the river. On either side of the dam they could see the tops of the intake towers through which passed the water that generated the electricity used for the huge steel plants of Pittsburgh. Jimmy Christopher pointed to the dam. "That's new, isn't it?" he asked Ericson.

Ericson nodded. "It was begun before the Purple Invasion, by the Federal Administration. Rudolph had it finished. It's one of the biggest dams on the Ohio—five hundred feet high. It will hold six million gallons of water. They had to finish it in order to get all their new plants going. It generates enough power to supply every need of the Purple Empire in the whole Pittsburgh district." Ericson went on bitterly: "They used American forced labor on that dam, Operator 5, and hundreds of men died while it was being built. Now it furnishes the power to make the guns that are going to crush us!"

"What is it called?" Jimmy asked.

"The Maximilian Dam," Ericson told him, "after Rudolph's father, Emperor Maximilian I."

They drove on past the huge Maximilian Dam, and then Ericson swung slightly to the left into what had once been California Avenue. Here, the tall spire of a church loomed darkly into the night, connected with half a dozen other buildings. This one spot had somehow been spared, as if by a miracle of God, from the bombardment of the Central Empire. Now it stood, deserted and lonely in the night.

Ericson pulled the truck a little past the group of buildings, and Jimmy Christopher dismounted. Diane Elliot and five of the men got out of the rear of the truck. Diane was carrying a long flambeau torch, which she had not yet lighted.

Jimmy said to Ericson: "Wait for us here. If you hear a patrol coming, sound your horn twice, but don't leave. If you just stay here, the patrol won't suspect you."

ERICSON NODDED, and Jimmy led the way, with Diane and the five men following into the deserted church building. He clicked on his flashlight, and they made their way up the narrow staircase of the church, into the steeple. Jimmy looked over the side.

To the right of the church building was the sloping roof of the rectory, pitch black in the night. He looked out across the Ohio River toward the airport where Ames' men were waiting for the signal, and nodded in satisfaction. "They should be able to see the torch from here." He turned around and addressed the small group: "This is a decisive moment in American history. We are about to give a signal that will launch rebellions in twenty-four cities. Thousands of men will die tonight—so that we can carry on our plan with a little greater chance for success. We must not fail those men who are dedicating their lives tonight! Now—"

He stopped as two short blasts of Eric-son's horn sounded in the night. Diane, who had already taken out a match with which to light the torch, exclaimed: "That's Ericson's signal. The patrol must be coming!"

Swiftly, Jimmy Christopher stepped to the parapet, and looked over. Sure enough, a patrol of four armored motorcycles was chugging down California Avenue toward them. Even as Jimmy watched, the four motorcycles pulled up short alongside the truck, and a sergeant called out: "Who is in charge of your truck?"

Ericson, who had said he was able to speak the language of the Central Empire, answered the sergeant. "I am in command, Sergeant. What is it you wish?"

Jimmy Christopher groaned, as he heard Ericson talk. The man could speak the language of the Central Empire all right, but his accent was atrocious. It was the one thing that Jimmy had forgotten to check. He had taken it for granted that Ericson spoke the language fluently, and had not thought of testing him on it.

That American accent was not lost upon the sergeant in charge of the motorcycles. He shouted: "Come down here. Show me your papers!"

Ericson must have lost his head. He yelled: "Damn you, come and get them!" And at the same time he drew his revolver.

The motorcycle patrol was equipped with side cars, and the trooper in each of the side cars had been holding a rifle ready. At Ericson's action they fired simultaneously, and Ericson slumped over the wheel, with a half dozen slugs in his body.

The Americans from inside the truck began to troop out, but they hadn't a chance. The small sub-machine guns mounted on the front of the motorcycles mowed them down like ninepins as they emerged. The staccato rattle of the machine guns filled the street with deafening noise as the Americans died under those deadly blasts.

The firing ceased almost as soon as it had begun. Inert bodies of the Americans lay sprawled on the snow, with blood rapidly spreading about them. Disaster had come unexpectedly, without notice, and had struck swiftly, mercilessly. In an instant of time hope was turned to despair.

One of the troopers in the motorcycle pointed excitedly up toward the steeple. He shouted to the sergeant, indicating the figures of Jimmy Christopher, Diane, and the Americans. The sergeant swore under his breath, issued quick orders, and the men dismounted from their motorcycles, raced across the street toward the church.

Jimmy Christopher swung around tensely. "Di! Light that torch. We've got to give the signal."

THEY HEARD running feet on the stairs below, and Jimmy quickly ordered two of the men to guard the stair-head. Diane was fumbling with matches, and she finally got the torch alight, reached out to wave it into the night. Rifle shots whined around her from the street below. Two of the troopers had remained down there, and were firing up.

Other troopers now appeared on the slanting roof of the rectory, running toward the steeple. Jimmy Christopher raced around to that side, drawing his revolver. The night grew raucous with the quick explosions of rifles and revolvers.

The two men at the stair-head fell, wounded, and two of the other Americans sprang to take their place. The last of the Americans rushed to Jimmy's assistance as he fired to check the Central Empire troopers who tried to climb over into the steeple.

Diane frantically waved the torch into the night, praying that the men at the airport would spot it.

The American beside Jimmy fell with a bullet wound in his forehead. Jimmy reached over and smashed the head of a Central Empire trooper who was clinging to the wall with one hand, and aiming at him with the other. The man's gun exploded into the air, and he fell back to the sloping roof, unconscious. The rectory roof was clear.

Jimmy Christopher swung around wildly, leaped to the assistance of the single man left defending the stair-head. Shots were coming up from down below, and even as Jimmy raced toward the stair-head, the last of the Americans fell, his body riddled with slugs.

Jimmy Christopher reached over, thrust his hand into the opening, and fired a steady stream of slugs down. A choked scream answered his fusillade, and the firing from below ceased. Jimmy poked his head into the opening. He was now clearly outlined against the sky behind him, but no shots greeted him. The last of the enemy had perished down there.

He turned swiftly at the sound of Diane's excited voice. "Jimmy! Look! They've seen the signal!"

Operator 5 leaped across to Diane's side. Sure enough, far in the distance they saw three rockets following one another in a tall arch across the sky!

The men at the airport had gotten the signal, and were relaying it across the country. The word was being spread, throughout the twenty-four cities, for the rebellion to begin.

No one seemed to have come to investigate the battle at the

church. They were a good distance above the outskirts of the city now, and this patrol of motorcycles must have been the only one in the neighborhood.

Jimmy Christopher snatched the torch from Diane's hand, stamped it out on the floor. Then he seized her hand, said: "Let's go, Di. We better get out of here before we're caught. We have work to do tonight!"

They raced down the stairs, and outside Jimmy stopped for a moment, looking somberly at the bodies of the dead Americans scattered on the ground. These men had died, because of a slight oversight. If Jimmy Christopher had only thought to make sure that Ericson could talk the language of the Central Empire without an accent, these men might still be alive.

Suddenly, Diane Elliot uttered a choked cry and ran toward the truck. She stooped, examined the riddled bodies of the dead Americans. "I can't find him, Jimmy. I can't find Tim."

Jimmy Christopher's blood suddenly ran cold. He had forgotten about Tim Donovan. The lad had been left in the truck with the other men. He must be dead, inside, for the canvas of the truck was riddled in many spots. At the thought that Tim Donovan might be dead, Jimmy Christopher suddenly felt a queer emptiness. His hands were clammy with sweat. He started toward the truck, reluctantly, almost fearful to look inside.

And just at that moment a small voice from behind him called out: "Never mind looking in there, Jimmy. Here I am."

Jimmy and Diane both whirled around, stood staring almost unbelievingly at the slight figure of Tim Donovan who was

DIANE

emerging from inside the church. There was a lump on the right side of the boy's head.

Diane uttered a sob, ran forward and hugged Tim close to her breast. "Timmy! What happened? Where—"

Tim Donovan said: "Aw, don't start babying me, Di. I couldn't stay in the truck, and wait while you went up in the church, so I followed you. I was just inside when those troopers came and got our men. Then they came into the church, and I saw you shooting down at them from upstairs, so I just took a pot shot at a couple of 'em from down below. That was me that shot the last guy on the stairs, when you poked your head out. He fell down, and landed right on top of me. He was still holding on to his gun, and I must have got a sock on the head. I guess I was out for a couple of minutes. I just came to as you and Jimmy were running out, and I managed to push the trooper off me, and get up."

"Thank God," Diane murmured fervently.

Jimmy Christopher put a hand on the boy's shoulder, pressed hard. "Okay, Tim, you lucky kid." That was all he needed to say. Tim Donovan knew just how he felt, and there was little need for exchange of sentiment between this man and this boy.

Operator 5 swung around, gazed solemnly at the dead bodies of the Americans sprawling on the snow. "We'll have to leave them here. There's no time to waste. Those rockets are going up all over the country, and soon the Central Empire will be moving troops out of here in all directions. We've got to carry on with the plan. I know these boys won't mind if we leave them."

For a moment they were silent while Diane's lips moved. Then Jimmy Christopher said briskly: "We'll take the motorcycles. They'll be more use to us tonight than the truck."

Each of them mounted one of the motorcycles, and the procession drove oft, leaving the bodies of the dead Americans staining the thick snow a deep carmine.

JIMMY DID not drive back toward the Experimental Building. The death of those twenty men had changed his plans. He could not now attempt to free Ransom without some assistance. So instead of heading for the Experimental Building, he drove southwest across the North Side Bridge, and into the devastated residential section of Pittsburgh. Here were neither buildings nor people, only the scattered ruins of what had once been a beautiful suburb. Ahead of them they could see the steep slope of Mount Washington Park, and at the top of it the concrete emplacements which the Central Empire had erected for the Big Berthas.

The single headlight of Jimmy Christopher's motorcycle suddenly outlined the figure of a Central Empire trooper standing in the road. The trooper stepped quickly back, out of the glare of the headlight, and Jimmy Christopher slowed up, came to a halt. The trooper advanced uncertainly, and Jimmy saw that it was one of Ames' men. Jimmy called out: "It's all right, friend."

Behind the American, Jimmy could see the huddled mass

of many people who had taken shelter in a group of ruins off the road.

The American in the uniform of the Central Empire trooper called out: "It's Operator 5!"

Jimmy Christopher raised his hand to Diane and Tim, then kicked his motorcycle into life again, cut off the road and across the snow-covered field toward the ruins where he could see the people huddling. He turned off his spotlight, and Diane and Tim did likewise. When they had pulled up close to the ruins, Frank Ames came out to meet them. Ames' forehead was wrinkled in puzzlement.

"What's happened, Operator 5?" he asked. "You weren't due here for another couple of hours—"

Swiftly Jimmy Christopher explained to him what had happened. "I've had to change my plans. We'll have to take the enemy position up there first, and get these women and children to a place of safety. Then we can go down and attempt to rescue Ransom. We'll try to free all those others, too."

"Do we go now?" Ames asked eagerly.

"No. We've got to wait several hours, until the news of the rebellions comes through. Then they'll begin shifting troops. We've got to give the troops enough time to get out of Allegheny County, and on the way toward the focuses of rebellion. Then we'll strike. Is it safe to remain here?"

Ames nodded. "The Central Empire troopers don't cover this district. Nobody's supposed to be here, and they don't pass this way on the way to the Mount Washington fortifications. They go across by the West Liberty Tunnel. We're fairly safe from observation, and if we post a guard along the road we can stay here for several hours without being noticed."

"How many people have you got here?"

"We've got about five hundred women and children, the families of many of the men who are working in the mills. We also have Ransom's two kids. A few of us went to the Detention Room, and we presented a forged order to the warden, commanding him to turn the prisoners over to us. He was suspicious, but it was too late. We overpowered him, and locked him and his keepers in the cells, and released all the women and children prisoners. They won't discover it until tomorrow morning, when the relief guard goes to the jail."

"Good man!" Jimmy Christopher said warmly. "That means that Franklin Ransom needn't be worried about his children any more. Now, if we can get him out of that Experimental Building, and get him back west of the Rockies with us, he can work out ransomite three for us."

TIM DONOVAN had been fooling around his motorcycles, and now he came running over to Jimmy Christopher, his young face flushed with excitement.

"Jimmy!" he gasped "I was tinkering with the two-way radio on that motorcycle, and I got in touch with Z-7. I've got contact now. He wants to talk to you. Come on."

Jimmy Christopher followed Tim to the motorcycle, and donned the ear-phones of the compact little two-way radio set, with which every mechanized unit of the Central Empire forces was equipped.

He said: "Z-7! This is O-5."

Z-7's voice came floating through the ether, accompanied by the crackling of static and the booming of big guns. "Jimmy! How are you making out!"

"I don't know yet, Z-7," Jimmy told him. "We're on the verge of carrying out the operation you know of. But I can't give you any further details, because we may be overheard. How is it out there?"

"It's bad, Jimmy, very bad. We can't hold for more than a day or two longer. Those big guns are pounding us to pieces, and we hear that they're bringing up more guns. They've leveled off Salt Lake City—there isn't one stone standing on another. I hope to God your plan proves successful."

"It's in the works now, Z-7," Operator 5 said. "We should have results before the night is over. Hold tight, sir. I'll talk to you again later."

He took off the ear-phones, and sat dejectedly on the edge of the motorcycle, looking at Tim. Then his gaze wandered up the slope of Mount Washington toward the fortifications at the top.

"Our one chance is that they haven't manned those fortifications yet. If we can only take them, we can make it hot enough for the Central Empire to compel them to draw in their troops from the Wasatch Range."

Tim Donovan was looking at him queerly. "Jimmy, there's something bothering you. Aside from the things that have happened tonight, you haven't been looking right. Tell me—have you got anything on your mind?"

Jimmy Christopher looked up at the boy. "On my mind?" He

tried to assume an air of innocence, as he saw Diane approaching them. "Why should I have anything on my mind?"

"I don't know," Tim kept on doggedly. "You've got something that's bothering you, aside from these things that we're up against over here. Come on now, come across. What is it?"

Diane's eyes were searching Jimmy's face. She put her hand on his arm "I—I know. It's about Nan and MacTavish. That's what's worrying you, isn't it, Jimmy? You don't know what's happened to them."

Jimmy bowed his head. "God help me, Di, I do know."

Tim and Diane drew closer to him. "Tell us," Diane breathed.

Jimmy Christopher closed his eyes hard, and spoke dully.

"Nan and MacTavish are to be executed tomorrow. They were captured in New York, and they escaped, but they were recaptured. The men they gathered for the rebellion were killed or arrested. Now Nan and MacTavish are in Rudolph's hands, and they're to be executed tomorrow. Nan is to be suspended from a gibbet opposite St. Patrick's Cathedral, *hanging head down*. And MacTavish—he's to be *crucified!*"

Tim Donovan and Diane Elliot looked at him in stunned silence.

Tim's small hand clenched at his side. "What—what are we going to do about it, Jimmy?"

"Nothing, Tim," Operator 5 told him bitterly. "We're going to do nothing at all about it."

Diane burst out: "But you can't leave them to die like that, Jimmy! We've got to try to save them—"

She stopped as Jimmy Christopher looked up at her with eyes that were filled with misery.

"No, Diane, we can't do a thing about it. Nan and MacTavish are only two—no matter how dear they are to us. There are thousands of Americans who are giving up their lives all over the country tonight, so that we can carry on this plan. And would you want me to leave all those thousands of men in the lurch in order to go and save my sister from death?"

Diane had no answer. Her hands were ripping her handkerchief to shreds, as she lowered her eyes so as not to see the agony in Jimmy Christopher's face.

CHAPTER 9
THE CORONATION EVE
REBELLIONS

THAT NIGHT, the torch which Diane Elliot had waved from the steeple of the abandoned church in Pittsburgh set afire the greatest spirit of self-sacrifice which had ever been witnessed in the history of any nation on the face of the earth.

Across the vast panorama of occupied America, rockets sped into the sky at intervals, and watching eyes spied them in the night, prepared for concerted action. Those rockets blazed over the distilleries of Kentucky, the coal district of Southern Illinois, the Missouri corn belt, the tobacco fields of Northern Tennessee and the rice fields of Arkansas; over the Chicago stock yards and over the wheat lands of Nebraska; over the destroyed oil lands of Oklahoma, and over the cattle ranges of Wyoming and Montana.

Wherever those rockets blazed, grim-faced men marched against their conquerors, using whatever weapons came to hand. Rebellion spread through the land—rebellion that was doomed to failure because of the miserable equipment of the Americans. They knew they were marching to death or worse; yet they went eagerly, willingly, prepared to give up their lives in order that Operator 5's desperate venture might succeed.

Only in Pennsylvania was there no sign of rebellion. And, as frantic commandants of the various occupied territories wired for planes and for more troops, column after column left Pennsylvania by rail and by truck to go to their assistance.

As if God Himself were favoring this gallant bid for freedom, a furious blizzard swept in over the Great Lakes, piling up drifts of snow, bogging down the Central Empire columns, freezing truck motors, and making the railroad tracks so slippery as to virtually stop the troop trains. Telegraph wires went down, and radio communication became almost impossible.

The waters of the Ohio River swelled and rolled in a thunderous charge against the mighty Maximilian Dam, just above Pittsburgh; but the huge structure of concrete and steel wire held firmly, penning in the angry waters. A little farther to the south, on the southern shore of the Monongahela River, the massive heights of the hilly residential section of Pittsburgh rose in frowning silence, overlooking the valley of the Golden Triangle across the river.

On the slope of those heights, in the Mount Washington

section, some five hundred shivering women and children huddled close together for warmth and protection against the biting cold and the howling winds. Above them, on the crest of Mount Washington heights, the concrete emplacements of the fortifications shone white in the moonlight, thinly covered with the first fall of snow. Below, and across the river, were visible the low, squat buildings where Franklin Ransom and the hundreds of other Americans were confined, and farther east could be seen the blazing funnels of the furnaces where iron was being converted into weapons of war.

Not far from where those women and children huddled together, Frank Ames stood in conference with Jimmy Christopher, Diane Elliot and Tim Donovan. Nearby some two hundred men—all that Ames had been able to recruit under the noses of the Central Empire patrols—stood waiting for the word that would launch them against the fortifications above. It was midnight, and they had waited here for four hours, while messengers came at intervals to report the departure of more and more Purple troops toward the areas where rebellion had sprung up.

A last messenger now approached them, working his way with difficulty along the road on foot, through the deepening snow. Wind tore against the messenger's face as he forced the words from his lips.

"I just saw the Twenty-fourth Purple Grenadiers entrain for the west, Operator 5," he reported. "That leaves hardly more than five hundred troops in the Pittsburgh area."

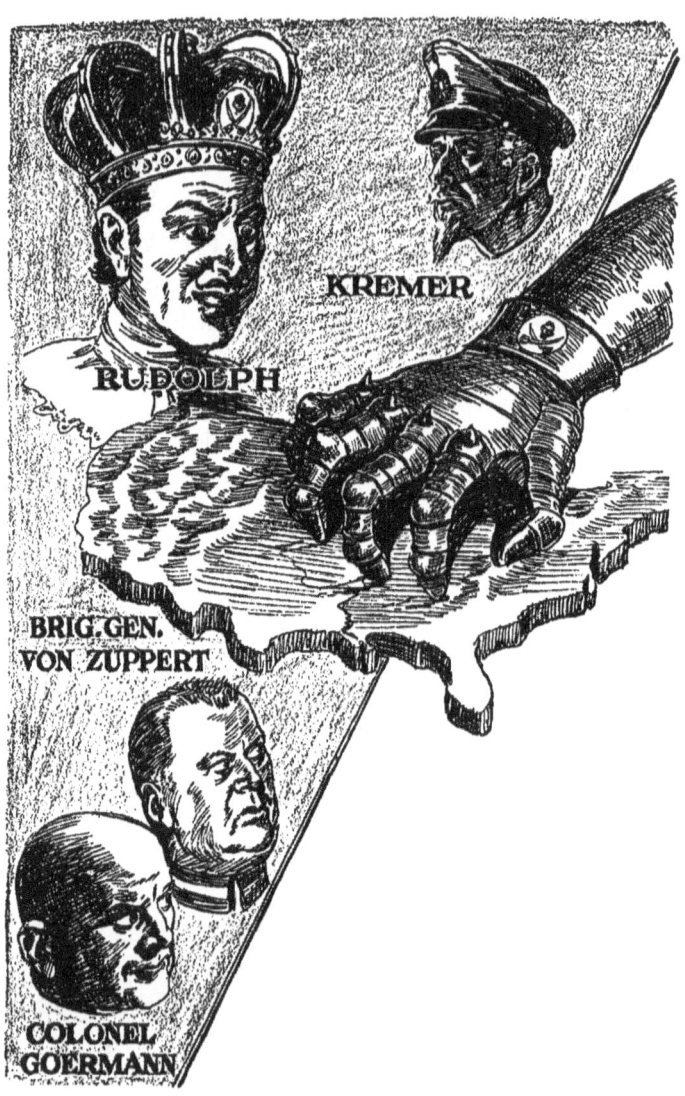

Jimmy Christopher nodded in satisfaction. "We can attack now," he said to Ames. "Give the signal."

FRANK AMES saluted briskly, and placed a whistle to his lips. He blew three short, sharp blasts upon it, and the waiting men snapped to attention. A low, muffled cheer ran down their ranks.

Jimmy Christopher stepped to the front, addressed the men shortly, raising his voice so as to be heard above the piercing shrieks of the wind:

"We're ready to go, men. There are about three hundred of the Purple troops up there in the fortifications. We're slightly outnumbered, but we've got to take that hill. Remember, thousands of Americans all over the country are giving up their lives to make this attack a success. For their sakes, we must not fail. That hill must be taken. Now, let's go!"

He led the way up along the rutted road that twisted toward the peak. The blizzard tore at them, fought to sweep them off the road; but they marched stubbornly on toward the top.

Behind them, many of the women detached themselves from the groups huddling among the ruins and followed the men. Many of these had rifles, sawed-off shotguns, and any other weapons which had been available. These women had been prisoners of the Central Empire, hostages for the good behavior of their husbands who were shackled in the mills down below. They were pale, hungry, for they had been treated with little consideration, and had been fed hardly at all by their captors.

Far from breaking their spirit, however, this treatment had fired within them the fierce desire to fight to the bitter end so that their children might not once more be subjected to the harsh imprisonment from which they had just been rescued.

It was a long, hard climb to the crest of the heights where the Central Empire fortifications were erected. The homes which had formerly dotted these slopes lay in ruins all about them. When the Central Empire had first taken Pittsburgh, the American defenders had retreated to the bluffs south of the Monongahela River, but the Purple Artillery had smashed them out, leaving no single building standing intact. Here and there a bit of wall still reared itself up into the night. In other places, dark, unmarked mounds of earth indicated where the bodies of brave patriots had been buried wholesale by the conquerors.

Some two hundred yards from the first breastwork of the fortifications, the ground had been entirely cleared, and the jotting rocks had been blasted away, leaving a level open space over which an attacker would ordinarily have to charge, becoming exposed to a withering fire from those breastworks. But now, no such fire greeted the advancing patriots, for the fortifications were not yet manned.

Operator 5 and Frank Ames, in the lead, pressed forward cautiously over the cleared ground, while the main body of Americans remained behind in the shelter of the ruins.

A single sentry, standing upon the first low breastwork, lackadaisically watched their approach. They were all in Central Empire uniforms, and the man entertained no thought that this might be an attack.

Ames whispered to Jimmy: "The main body of the garrison will probably be all the way up at the top there, where you see that low concrete structure. If we can get past this sentry without alarming them, we can take them by surprise."

Jimmy nodded. His eyes were sweeping across the elaborate fortifications here. If only they could take this position, they could hold it indefinitely provided that their ammunition and food and water held out. The breastworks were arranged in a series of six, one behind the other, reaching up to the summit where the concrete shed-like structure sat, commanding the entire slope. Behind the third, fourth, fifth and sixth embankments were concrete gun emplacements, from which the long snouts of huge cannon projected.

Each of the concrete breastworks rose higher than the one before it, so that upon falling back from the first line, the defenders could command that first line from behind the second breastwork, and so on, until they reached the fort itself. From the roof of the fort, Jimmy could see the long thin muzzles of anti-aircraft guns.

Ames said to him: "I talked secretly to some of the Americans who were employed on this project. They tell me that the whole fortification is honeycombed with underground trenches and subterranean passages. These outer breastworks are really only the first line of defense. If this position were properly manned by a thousand men, it could almost never be taken."

NOW THEY were within twenty feet of the sentry, and the man stood stiffly at attention, saluted upon seeing Jimmy Christopher's major's uniform.

Jimmy threw back a low word of command, and Ames and the others of the small group halted while Jimmy himself approached the sentry. Behind them, no sound or movement indicated that the main body of attackers was hidden among the scattering ruins of the cliffside.

The sentry said mechanically: "Advance, sir, and be pleased to give the password of the day."

Jimmy Christopher did not know the password of the day. He frowned at the man as if in disapproval, and stepped closer. The sentry looked puzzled, and started to swing his rifle down with the bayonet pointing at Operator 5. Jimmy reached out with a sudden, swift movement, seized the barrel of the man's rifle, and yanked it hard.

The man uttered a cry of surprise as he was dragged forward. Jimmy let go of the rifle, and swung a hard fist to the man's jaw. The sharp snap of the blow was drowned by the howling of the wind, and the sentry crumpled to the snow without a sound.

Jimmy stood still for a moment, tautly holding the rifle, waiting to see if his action had been observed from the inner breastworks. But apparently this was the only sentry who was stationed here for the night. It was not strange that this should be so, for an attack at this place, in the center of the enemy territory, was unthinkable. This lone sentry had no doubt been placed here only as a matter of form.

Operator 5 left the unconscious sentry to lie in the snow, and stepped through the gate in the breastworks, followed by Ames and a half dozen other men.

Jimmy whistled with surprise as he gazed at the defense preparations behind this outer breastworks. There was a space of some hundred yards between the first and the second embankments. A concrete bed had been laid across this entire strip, and there were five dome-like structures studded about in this open space, each about five feet in height. Each of these structures had loopholes for machine guns. It was obvious that any attacker could be mowed down mercilessly by the guns from those five domes—if he should ever succeed in crossing the breastworks.

Ames said bitterly: "There's the latest in machine-gun nests. Our own men were forced to build these. It's an almost impregnable fortress!"

In the center of this wide concrete floor, studded with machine-gun nests, a narrow ramp led down into the bowels of the earth. Ames pointed to it, said: "That's the entrance to their underground stronghold. It connects all the way through, by passages, with the main fort."

Jimmy Christopher ordered him swiftly: "Bring up your men, Ames. We'll attack through those passages."

Ames turned, raised his arm in the air, and slowly the dark, shadowy figures of his men detached themselves from the ruins below, and crept up over the breastworks.

OPERATOR 5 led the way down the ramp, into a wide chamber cut out of the natural rock. He stopped a moment here, staring in amazement at the vast amount of work that had been put into this project.

Spiral staircases led up to platforms in the roof, where the machine guns were mounted under the low domes which they had seen from above. The cleverness of this arrangement was apparent. If an attacking force should storm the first line of breastworks, and sweep down this ramp, those machine guns on

113

the platforms could be swung about to mow down the enemy in this chamber.

Piled in orderly array along all the walls were crate upon crate of machine gun ammunition, hand grenades and flame bombs.

A passage at the far end led into another chamber, which was apparently under a similar concrete floor behind the second row of breastworks. Thus, Jimmy Christopher proceeded at the head of his men from chamber to chamber until they had traversed six of them. They were moving constantly upward in a gentle slope, and they finally reached the last subterranean chamber, which Ames told him was directly underneath the fort.

In each of the last three chambers were huge blocks of concrete, some fifteen feet in height, upon which had been set the huge Big Berthas about which they had heard so much. The guns were so placed that the breech and the loading mechanism was all below ground, and the only thing which projected above the concrete ceiling through a narrow porthole was the long muzzle. The guns rode on tracks, which were cunningly arranged with a series of rubber cushions to take up the recoil.

Jimmy Christopher had not stopped to examine these Big Berthas as they passed, but Ames had told him that those guns were actually light enough to be transported by trucks. They would, of course, have to be mounted upon emplacements in order to be fired, but the Central Empire was hoping to overcome even that obstacle through the invention of ransomite three.

So far they had encountered none of the enemy in these subterranean chambers. But now as they reached the last chamber, Jimmy Christopher stopped short at sight of the sentry on duty at the foot of the ramp leading up into the fort. Several arched doorways led off into barrack rooms on either side, and Jimmy could see Central Empire troopers in those rooms, seated about tables, playing games and conversing in loud and raucous voices.

The sentry's eyes opened wide in astonishment as he saw the large force of men who poured into the room after Operator 5. Many of Ames' men were in Central Empire uniforms, but the additional men whom he had recruited after returning to the city still wore civilian clothes. The sentry was plainly puzzled.

Before he could act, Jimmy Christopher stepped up close to him and pressed a revolver into the man's side.

"Silence, my friend," he said in the language of the Central Empire.

The sentry froze, staring into Jimmy's face in unbelief. Jimmy raised a hand, motioned toward the barrack rooms.

The Americans under Ames swarmed in among the Central Empire troopers. Jimmy disarmed the sentry as shouts and sounds of fighting came from the barrack rooms. The Central Empire soldiers had been taken completely by surprise, and many of them were unarmed. In a few moments they were subdued.

Operator 5 turned the sentry over to one of the Americans, then separated a group of some fifty men, and led the way up the ramp into the fort itself.

The fighting down below had given warning to the men above, and Jimmy Christopher was met at the head of the ramp by a uniformed officer and a squad of men. The officer shouted: "Who goes there?" and raised his gun.

Jimmy called to him: "Lay down your arms and surrender. You are outnumbered. We are Americans!"

The Central Empire officer snarled his defiance, and pressed the trigger of his gun. But Jimmy Christopher fired first, and the officer was hurled backward by the impact of the shot, to stagger against his own squad of troopers. The Purple soldiers turned to flee in panic before the furious charge of the Americans, and Jimmy's patriots uttered loud shouts of victory as they swarmed all over the fort, making prisoners of the demoralized Central Empire troops.

In less than five minutes the fort was theirs.

NOW JIMMY CHRISTOPHER superintended the work of bringing in the women and children. The captured Purple troopers were herded into a single room, disarmed, and locked in. The women and children took possession of the sleeping quarters, and Operator 5 quickly assigned position to all of his men. Nor did he leave the outer breastworks undefended. He sent men to man the machine-gun nests, and he also placed half a dozen look-outs at the first line of defense. In less than an hour he had organized the fort on a fighting basis.

The Americans were jubilant, and throughout the fort and the subterranean chambers the strains of the Star Spangled Banner rang out in a spontaneous, stentorian outburst, as the Purple flag was hauled down, and the Stars and Stripes rose above the fort.

Twenty experienced gunners took charge of the Big Berthas, and began to ransack the store rooms for ammunition.

Tim Donovan investigated the various cubbyholes and small rooms in the main building until he found the radio room. He set to work at once, trying to get into communication with Z-7, while Operator 5 led Frank Ames and Diane, together with half a dozen of the junior officers of the American force into the Commandant's office.

Ames' face was flushed with success.

"We've put it over, Operator 5," he exulted. "We've got the fort. Now we can blast those factories and steel mills out of existence. We can cripple the Central Empire's source of munitions—"

"You forget," Jimmy Christopher broke in dryly, "that there are a lot of our men chained in those mills. We've got to get them out before we can turn these guns on the factories. And we want Franklin Ransom, too. I'm going to put you in charge of this place, Ames. You will be the Commanding Officer. I'll take twenty-five men, and go down to the Experimental Building. If I don't return in two hours, start your bombardment of the valley. It'll mean that I've either failed or am dead."

Ames said soberly: "If you're going down there to rescue Ransom, why don't you let somebody else do it? Why not let me take the detail for that job—"

Jimmy Christopher shook his head. "As Major von Innsbruck, I have the entrée to that building. I'm the logical one to do it."

He turned to Diane Elliot, who had stood quietly listening. "You, Di, take charge of the women and children down below. Keep them quiet, and tell them not to worry about their men-folk. Arrange for food for them as well as the garrison, and provide sleeping quarters for everyone."

Diane nodded wordlessly.

Ames said: "I'll get your twenty-five men ready, Operator 5," and left the room.

Just then Tim Donovan came in from the radio room. The boy's face was flushed. "I've contacted Z-7, Jimmy, and he says there's five feet of snow in the Wasatch Mountains. The snow has stopped the advance of the Central Empire, but it hasn't stopped their artillery. They're battering at our positions, and Z-7 says he may have to pull out by tomorrow. He's been getting reports from all over the country. There've been rebellions in most of the key cities right across the face of the map. The whole country is in turmoil, and troops are being rushed to every point where there are uprisings. In a couple of the cities the rebellions have been quelled, but in most of the others they're still raging."

Operator 5 nodded. "So far, so good, Tim. You remain here at the radio. I'm going to raid the valley—"

"Wait a minute, Jimmy, there's more news," Tim Donovan went on. "It seems that the Canadians have been raising an army up around Georgian Bay, across from Mackinac Island. The army is under command of the Canadian general, Sir John Batten. There was so much static due to the storm that I couldn't get everything Z-7 told me, but it sounded as if Sir John Batten is embarking his army on a small fleet of boats across Lake Ontario, and is going to land them near Rochester. I don't know if Z-7 said he was going to do it, or had already done it."

Jimmy Christopher seized Tim Donovan's shoulders. "You

mean that Sir John Batten is marching right into the occupied territory? The man's crazy!"

Tim Donovan grinned up at Operator 5. "No crazier than you, Jimmy. You think you're the only one who has a right to do daffy things?"

Jimmy Christopher frowned. "You've got to find out more about that army, Tim. Get on the radio. Keep working it every minute. Get all the information you can, and have it ready for me when I come back from the Experimental Building!"

He kissed Diane lightly on the lips, shook hands with Tim, and went out to take charge of the men whom Ames had assembled for him.

AMES SAID excitedly: "We've, discovered something else about this place, Operator 5. There are four fast scout planes hangared behind the fort."

"Four planes?" Jimmy asked perplexedly. "How do they take off?"

"There's a retractable runway built out from the edge of the cliff, with a catapult to launch the plane."

"Good. See if any of your men have had experience as mechanics. If you find any, have them service the planes and get them ready for action. Then pick out some men who can fly. Those ships may prove valuable."

"Right, Operator 5," Ames said. "I'll take care of that. We've got the big guns all ready. We've only been able to dig up twenty shells for the Big Berthas, but that'll be enough to start with. I've got the men checking through all the supplies to find more shells."

119

Jimmy frowned. "I hope they find more. It would be too bad if we weren't able to use those guns."

He took his twenty-five men, and led them out across the breastworks and down the slope of the hill. These men were all dressed in the uniforms of the Central Empire, and Jimmy had seen to it that they were equipped with the new flame bombs which they had found in the fortifications.

Down at the river bank they commandeered one of the trucks in which Ames had transported the women and children refugees, and Jimmy Christopher deputized one of the men to drive, sitting beside the driver himself.

The cold had become intense, but the blizzard had let up in its fury. The solid tires of the truck crunched through the newly fallen snow, and Jimmy Christopher looked out over a white countryside, which appeared deceptively peaceful in the moonlight. To the right, across the Ohio River, they could still see the flaming stacks of the blast furnaces, and the long low piles of the squat shops.

They swung across the North Side Bridge, about half a mile below the towering structure of the Maximilian Dam. Then they swung back, making their way through what had formerly been known as Allegheny Town, and crossed the Allegheny River into the Golden Triangle. Now they were once more in front of the Experimental Building, and the driver pulled up to a halt.

Jimmy Christopher stared suspiciously at the entrance of the building where a guard of some fifteen men were stationed. The last time he had been there had been only a single sentry at the door. He wondered why the guard had been increased.

As he watched, he saw the sergeant in charge of the guard whisper to one of the men, and then saw the man turn and enter the Experimental Building. There was only one explanation for the mysterious actions of the guard.

Jimmy had known that his impersonation of Major von Innsbruck might be discovered at any time. If that were the case, then Colonel Goermann must be laying a trap for him. Swiftly his eyes darted from side to side. Some hundred yards past the Experimental Building he spotted the glint of a machine gun, mounted off to the side of the road. And beyond the machine gun, he noted the reflection of the moonlight on the keen edges of bayoneted rifles.

It was a trap.

Over his shoulder he called to the men inside the truck: "We're in a spot, boys. When I blow the whistle, you swarm out of the back of that truck, and charge at the door of the building."

He stopped, picked up four of the small flame bombs which he had placed at his feet in the truck. He held three of them in his left hand, the fourth in his right, and stepped swiftly down to the ground. As he did so, he saw the sergeant in charge of the guard raise his hand as if in signal toward the machine gun nest.

Almost at once a short, staccato burst of tracer bullets whined through the night, about ten feet to his right. The gunner was swiftly moving his muzzle to cut down Jimmy Christopher. Jimmy hurled his flame bomb, and then snatched the whistle from his pocket, blew a sharp blast.

The bomb landed accurately in front of the machine gun and a living wall of flame suddenly licked up toward the gun. These flame bombs had been developed by the Central Empire until they were a deadly menace. The chemicals which those bombs contained formed a flame so fierce that it could twist the hardened metal of gun into a shriveled mass of slag. As the flames enveloped the machine gun, the gunners shrieked in terror and fled, and the bullets ceased to beat their swift *rat-tat-tat.*

In answer to Jimmy's whistle, the Americans from inside the truck swarmed out, with fixed bayonets, and charged the guard at the door.

Jimmy Christopher sent another flame bomb hurtling down the road in the direction of the gleaming bayonets he had seen, then he drew his revolver and raced to the aid of the men at the doorway.

THE CENTRAL EMPIRE troopers had been smugly expecting to catch the Americans in a deadly trap. They were stunned and surprised by the swiftness of the counter-attack. The American bayonets flashed in and out with merciless purpose, and the alien troopers fled before the wild attack.

Jimmy Christopher pushed through the men, raced through the doorway and into the open-hearth shops. Panicky guards attempted to bar their path, but the Americans behind Jimmy were in too fierce a mood to be stopped by anything.

And the civilian workers leaped up as far as their shackles would permit, and grappled with the Central Empire guards, preventing them from firing at the attackers. Jimmy Christopher raced down the entire length of that building, with the wild shouts of the civilians ringing in his ears, followed by his men.

He reached the room where he knew Franklin Ransom to be, and his swift glance took in the situation in an instant.

Henry Daws lay dead across the desk, with a bullet hole in his brain. Colonel Goermann faced Franklin Ransom, who was straining at the shackles which held him to the bench. A dozen of Goermann's troopers were between the Colonel and the doorway. The Central Empire soldiers had removed the bayonets from their rifles, and were holding their guns ready to fire.

Jimmy Christopher moved fast. He hurled one of his flame bombs directly at the troopers. It struck the floor, and burst into a sheet of fire from which the troopers retreated with screams of panic.

Goermann was also caught behind that wall of flame, and he was forced back into a corner of the room with his troopers.

Jimmy Christopher leaped to Ransom's side, shouted: "Let's go, Mr. Ransom. I'll shoot your shackles off—"

Ransom shook his head. "You can't do it, Operator 5. They're made of ransomite two. Only a special chemical will weaken them sufficiently to break."

"Good God!" exclaimed Jimmy. "How'll we get out of here?"

The sizzling flame from the bomb was causing the temperature of the room to rise even higher than it had been before from the heat of the open hearth in the next room. Goermann and his troopers were firing through the flames in the direction of Jimmy and Ransom, and Operator 5 forced the inventor down on his knees to avoid the bullets.

Jimmy inspected swiftly the shackles which held Ransom to the girder along the wall His eyes moved down the length of the girder, and narrowed speculatively as he saw that the steel beam was fastened to the wall by one huge bolt at either end.

"I'll be right back!" he shouted to Ransom, and weaved his way out of the room. His own men had not come in with him, but were busily moving about, shooting off the shackles of the American civilians. Apparently these shackles were not made of ransomite, for they broke under the impact of the gun shots. Many of the civilians already freed were smashing the machinery in the room. Jimmy Christopher seized one of these by the shoulder, swung him around. "An acetylene torch!" he shouted. "Quick. Where can I get one?"

The man shouted back: "Right here!" and led him to a tool closet at the end of the room. In a moment the man had taken out a complete acetylene torch equipment on rollers. "What do you want to do with this?"

"Follow me!" Jimmy ordered, and ran back toward the Experimental Room. He pointed out the bolts at either end of the beam, and the man nodded in swift understanding, set to work to shear those bolts with the acetylene torch.

The sizzling flames which kept Goermann and the troopers in the corner of the room were dying down, and Jimmy Christopher hurled another bomb onto the floor, close enough to pen them in, but not close enough to injure them. He could not find it in him to destroy these men with fire, even though they were willing to do the same to Americans, as was evidenced by their possession of the flame bombs at the fort.

The renewed flame from the second bomb served to keep them penned in, and their shots were ineffective, for the man who worked the acetylene torch, as well as Ransom and Jimmy, were shielded from them by the work bench.

THE TORCH sheared through the bolts at both ends as if they had been so much butter. The steel girder fell away from the wall, and Jimmy raced through the doorway, yelled to half a dozen of the men to come in. They lifted the girder, began to carry it out through the doorway in its entirety, with Ransom lying across it.

Now they were exposed to the fire from the troopers, and Jimmy Christopher covered the movements of the men who were carrying the girder by emptying his automatic into the flames. He did not know how many men he had hit, but he succeeded in silencing their fire long enough to enable the others to get through the doorway with the girder.

The Experimental Building, completely cleared of troopers, was in the hands of the civilians, who swarmed around them to lend a hand with the girder. The heavy steel beam was carried outside, and loaded onto the truck, which sped away into the night, with the liberated civilians crowded into its interior and hanging onto the running board on the outside.

Inside that truck, Jimmy Christopher was kneeling beside Franklin Ransom.

"Your formula for ransomite?" Jimmy asked eagerly. "You can reproduce it?"

Ransom nodded. "Give me a laboratory, and two hours to work, and I'll reproduce it. I had it all ready, but I was hold-ing back, in the hope that something like this would happen. But—tell me—where are you taking me? There is no place to go. We're in the heart of the enemy territory. How could we ever get through?"

Jimmy Christopher laughed harshly. "We've captured the enemy fortifications on Mount Washington. We're going up there. We can hold that spot against the whole Central Empire for a long time. You'll be able to work out your formula, all right."

The truck did not return at once to the fort. Instead, rifles and grenades were handed out to the civilians who had been rescued from the Experimental Building, and they were dropped off at intervals wherever the lights of a shop showed in the darkness.

These men were determined to rescue their fellow workers in those other shops, and lead them back to Mount Washington. Now that they were freed of their shackles, and had been informed that their families were safe in the fortifications, nothing, Jimmy Christopher was sure, would stop them. They were eager to come to grips with troopers of the Central Empire; anxious to avenge upon those men the humiliations and the tortures which they had suffered while shackled in the factory. And though they were clad only in trousers and undershirts, they did not mind the bitter cold—were hardly even aware of the weather. Their blood was on fire for revenge.

In the whole of Pittsburgh there were hardly more than five hundred troops left, and these were without effective command because Colonel Goermann was not able to issue orders. Jimmy Christopher did not know it, but one of his slugs had found the Colonel's heart through the flame. And the Central Empire troops were able to offer only a sporadic resistance to the half-naked madmen who attacked the other shops. In an hour every civilian had been freed from the huge plants in and around Pittsburgh. Trucks, cars and motor lorries were commandeered to carry them across the Allegheny to the Mount Washington fortifications.

Operator 5 had not waited for them to complete their task.

With his original twenty-five men, he drove back to the fort with Franklin Ransom in the truck.

It was a difficult task to carry that heavy steel girder up the steep incline, but they managed it, and bore Ransom into the fortifications.

It was good to see the Stars and Stripes waving over that impregnable fortress. Jimmy was weary from the exertion of the last hour, but he experienced a rejuvenation of spirit upon seeing the good old flag whipping in the wind.

Ames had done a good job of organizing the defense. He had optimistically expected Jimmy to succeed in the undertaking of rescuing the shackled civilians from the shops, and he had already divided his own men into skeleton companies into which he was able to fit the civilians, under experienced officers. The machine-gun nests were fully equipped with ammunition, and the Big Berthas were all ready to begin the bombardment of the valley. The only fly in the ointment was that they had not been able to locate more than the twenty original shells. Even at that, Ames was cheerful.

"These men will fight like the very devil," he told Operator 5. "Even without the Big Berthas, we can hold this fort till doomsday."

"What about food and water?" Jimmy asked.

Jimmy hurled a second flame bomb, penning Goermann and his

troopers, while his own men bore Ransom to safety.

"There's enough to last a thousand men for months. There's canned food, and water in casks. But it'll be tough on the children, because there's no milk. There's a small supply of evaporated milk, which I've set aside for the exclusive use of the children, but after that's gone, I don't know what we'll do."

TIM DONOVAN came into the Commandant's office, and broke into the conversation without so much as a by-your-leave. "Jimmy! That Canadian Army under Sir John Batten—I got some more dope on it. They landed outside Rochester yesterday, and they're marching down toward the Finger Lakes region. Z-7 has been in contact with them over the radio, but I can't raise a connection with them. Z-7 says Sir John Batten has raised a whole regiment of cavalry. I don't know how they'll make out in the snow—"

"Good God!" Jimmy Christopher exclaimed, "it's suicide to march toward the Finger Lakes region. The Central Empire has established a training camp headquarters there, and Batten will run into frightful odds. He'll be wiped out.

"You've got to reach him, Tim, head him off. He should swing west, and march through Chautauqua, then down into Pennsylvania. The purple troops have been pulled out of that territory to take care of the rebellions, and he'd have a fairly easy job of it except for the oil fields around Bradford, which Rudolph has fortified fairly well. Hurry, Tim. Get on the radio—"

Tim Donovan shook his head. "Can't do it, Jimmy. I've tried for a whole hour, and I can't raise him. Z-7 has also been out of touch with him since this afternoon."

"How many men has Batten with him, besides the regiment of cavalry?"

"I don't know exactly, but I think Z-7 said something about it being up to the strength of a full war time division." Operator 5 groaned. "They'll be wiped out at Finger Lakes, and we could use him to such good advantage down here." Suddenly Jimmy Christopher's eyes flashed with resolution. I'm going to find Batten!"

He swung around to Ames. "Order one of those scout planes made ready. I'm taking off in ten minutes."

"But we need you here!" Ames protested. The civilians are beginning to trickle in from the valley now, and it's going to be a big job to organize them. Besides, you wouldn't have much of a chance of getting through in this weather—"

"Nevertheless, I'm going," Jimmy said with finality. "It's worth the chance to increase our force by a whole division of fighting men. Do as I say, Ames. Have the plane made ready."

Ames looked helplessly at Tim, who shrugged, then grinned. "It's no use, Mr. Ames. When Operator 5 sets his mind on something, you might as well quit arguing. Better go get the plane ready."

Ames sighed, saluted, and left.

Jimmy Christopher gave Tim Donovan swift instructions. "Hang on to that radio every minute of the night, Tim. I'll try to keep in touch with you by radio from the plane. Tell Ames to begin the bombardment of the valley as soon as all the civilians are up here. He has only twenty shells for the big guns, and not a single one must be wasted.

131

"As for the defense of this fort, he's got to be prepared for an attack within a day or so. As soon as the Central Empire learns that we are in possession of this place, they'll bring troops up from Virginia and Jersey, and down from New York and New Hampshire. It's too bad that there aren't other guns besides those Big Berthas. He'll have to rely on the machine guns and hand grenades. No doubt the enemy will bring up heavy artillery of their own, and lay down a barrage on the hill.

"I think these concrete emplacements are strong enough to withstand any but the biggest guns. The enemy will probably lay down a furious barrage, and then send their infantry in. When the infantry comes, tell Ames to line the first embankment with men who are well supplied with hand grenades. Each breastwork must be fought independently, and must be kept to the last moment.

"Use the flame bombs too. And don't feel any compunctions about it. The enemy would use them without hesitation."

He shook hands with Tim, and left the room. Outside, he met Ames returning to inform him that the plane was ready.

"I've given Tim some last-minute instructions, which he will relay to you," Operator 5 told Ames. "I'll keep in touch with you by radio from the plane on the way up, as well as on the way down, after I find Sir John Batten. If he has a strong enough force, we'll smash our way into you, no matter who's in the way. If we're outnumbered, we may have to resort to some other strategy. Whatever happens, though, *hold the fort!*"

Jimmy Christopher left Ames watching him, and made his way to the rear of the cliff, where he climbed into the cockpit of the light cruising plane which had been made ready for him on the retractable runway. He gunned the motor and smiled in grim satisfaction at the sweet music it made. He raised his hand, and a man released the lever which set the catapult into action. The plane was hurled down the runway at a speed of eighty miles an hour, and took off gracefully, banking around toward the north.

As he faced grimly into the night, with the slipstream whipping around his head, he wondered if he had been right in doing this. Should he have remained with the defenders of the fort, rather than go on this undertaking? Yet, he could not allow the Canadian Division to march to its doom. The acquisition of that division would be of supreme importance to the American forces, and might even form the nucleus of a great thrust directly in the heart of the enemy territory.

CHAPTER 10
THE CANADIANS ARE
COMING!

WHITE SNOW lay deep upon the highroad which skirted the shores of Seneca Lake between Geneva and Penn Yan. But for a good stretch along that road, the whiteness of the snow was obscured by the dark figures of marching men and moving trucks. Sir John Batten's Canadian Division was marching south, right in the heart of the Finger Lakes section.

So far they had encountered no opposition, but at the southern end of Seneca Lake they would run into the first encampment of the Purple Army which was bivouacked in winter quarters in the State Park there.

This section of New York State had been laid waste in the early days of the Purple Invasion, as far west as Buffalo, and they had encountered hardly a soul on their march from Lake Ontario. Emboldened by this lack of opposition, they had lost much of their caution, and were marching with a view to speed rather than safety.

Thus it was that no one in the vanguard of that long column noted the lone airplane that dipped out of the sky directly toward them, until it was almost within shooting range. There were a dozen trucks in the lead, and behind them rode an endless line of cavalry, mounted upon the spirited little mustangs of the Canadian plains.

At the head of the cavalry regiment rode Sir John Batten himself, disdaining to sit at ease in a staff car or truck, and preferring to share the hardships of his pet cavalry regiment.

Sir John was a dapper, lithe man in his middle forties, and he rode with all the expertness of a sportsman. It was he who first spotted the plane, and noted the sinister insignia of the crossed broadswords and the severed head emblazoned upon the under side of the wing. He shouted swift orders, and two of the leading trucks pulled off the road, while the men in charge of them whipped off the tarpaulins, revealing two anti-aircraft guns. These were the only two which Sir John Batten had been able to find, and he wasn't even sure how they would work, for they were antiquated models which had been brought home from the World War by a Canadian regiment.

Now his men hastened to set the guns, and Sir John himself rode forward to give the order to fire. But looking up at the plane, he suddenly shouted: "Wait, men! Hold your fire!—"

For he could see that the pilot was leaning far out over the side of his cockpit, and waving a white handkerchief. They waited, puzzled, while the plane banked into the wind, and came down in a perfect three-point landing upon the frozen surface of the lake.

They stared in amazement as the aviator leaped from the cockpit, raced across the ice toward the road.

Sir John Batten frowned, and urged his horse over to meet the aviator. He said suspiciously: "Who are you? Why the white flag? If you have a message—"

He stopped short, staring in amazement at the face of the aviator. "Well, by all the gods! Without that moustache, I'd say you were Jimmy Christopher!"

Operator 5 smiled. "Right again, Sir John."

These two had met in Brussels, when Sir John was the Chief of British Espionage in that city, and Jimmy Christopher represented the United States Intelligence Bureau. A great respect for each other had grown up between these two, and had lasted over the years, though they had not seen each other for a long time. Sir John leaped from his horse, shook Jimmy's hand heartily. "By all the gods! What brings you here, togged out like one of those Purple swine? I heard this afternoon that you were having a devil of a time somewhere around Pittsburgh."

"Look here, Sir John," Operator 5 exclaimed. "I'll tell you all about Pittsburgh later. Right now, there's something more important on my mind. Do you know that you're marching right into the most powerful concentration of enemy troops east of the Rockies?"

"No!" Sir John Batten said almost unbelievingly. "Why, this territory is all devastated—"

"Quite so, but not down at the Watkins Glen State Park. That's where the enemy troops are concentrated. You're marching right into their mouths."

Sir John Batten turned pale. "What'll we do, then?"

"I suggest, sir, that you head west, through Hammondsport and Hornell, then south and across the Pennsylvania State Line. We'll meet a little opposition there, but not as much as you would hit here. And once we're through the enemy defenses around the oil fields in Northern Pennsylvania, your division will be a great help to me. By starting a number of rebellions throughout the country, I've caused the enemy to withdraw almost all of their troops from Pennsylvania. With this division, we could drive the enemy out of the state, and hold it against them."

Sir John Batten's eyes flashed with enthusiasm. "Good! We hadn't hoped for any such good fortune. We were merely marching down into America, with the hope of doing as much damage as we could before we were annihilated. We couldn't stand the inactivity of living up there in the Dominion, with all the fighting going on south of the border. Now that you give us a chance to do something useful, I'm sure we'll all be grateful!"

"Have some men trundle my plane on to a truck," Jimmy

Christopher directed. "I'll ride with you. It's been a long time since I had the pleasure of riding with a cavalry regiment!"
OPERATOR 5 discovered after the first day of the march, that Sir John Batten,* while a brave and courageous soldier, was not a good executive. He had imbued his men with a spirit of enthusiasm and sacrifice, which had carried them across the Great Lakes and into this enemy territory. He was prepared to die with them, if necessary.

But he had overlooked such important matters as providing adequate supplies. The rations gave out long before they reached the Pennsylvania border, and they were forced to send foraging parties on long trips to secure provisions.

In addition to the regiment of cavalry, there were two regiments of so-called motorized infantry, and a mixed regiment

---

* AUTHOR'S NOTE: The March of Sir John Batten's Canadian Division will always occupy a prominent spot in American history, and will forever remain as one of the major links in the lasting friendship between the United States and its northern neighbor. The epic tale of how that cavalry regiment struggled over two hundred miles of snow and ice through enemy territory deserves first place in any narrative of the Purple Invasion.

Ordinarily a journey that might have been accomplished by train overnight, this march occupied a full nine days. Two minor engagements with enemy scouting forces enlivened the first few days. But it was not until the fifth day that they crossed the State Line into Pennsylvania and met the full strength of the enemy's battalions. The oil country around Bradford had been rebuilt, and encircled with a ring of steel to protect it against sabotage by the Americans.

consisting of volunteers from every part of Canada. The motorized infantry was merely a makeshift arrangement. Every type of conveyance was in use, from five-ton Mack trucks to motorcycles with sidecars. There were some old Fords of such ancient vintage that one of them actually fell apart on the road. The supply of gasoline was limited, and it soon became apparent that the motorized infantry would either have to walk, or remain behind.

Jimmy Christopher rode a borrowed horse at the head of the column, beside Sir John. He was more than a bit morose. He did not wish to hurt Sir John Batten's feelings, but this Canadian division was a sore disappointment to Jimmy Christopher.

It was far from the fault of the Canadians, for no one could have expected them to manufacture gasoline and supplies. And the men themselves more than made up for their lack of equipment by the willingness and the courage which they showed. Many a truck was perforce abandoned at the roadside because of lack of fuel, and the men either doubled up on one of the other trucks, or trudged stubbornly on through the snow. Apparently there was no thought of retreat in their minds. They had set out to strike a blow at the conquerors, and they would do so even at the price of their lives.

The cavalry regiment alone was well groomed and well cared for. The men of this regiment were volunteers, and they had supplied their own mounts in many cases. Sir John, himself a noted sportsman, had contributed eighteen thoroughbreds to the regiment. Others had done likewise, and many of these men had not only brought their own horses, but had also supplied fodder for them.

Operator 5's plane had had to be abandoned, because there was no truck large enough to carry it, in spite of the fact that it was a very small scout plane. With the shortage of gasoline, it was useless for Jimmy to attempt to fly the plane with the column. So he had deliberately wrecked it, but had salvaged the two-way radio set, which he had caused to be set up in one of the trucks.

He maintained constant communication with both Z-7 at the Wasatch Mountains, and with Ames and Tim Donovan in Pittsburgh. From these two sources he heard much bad news, and a little that was good.

He learned that the enemy artillery was decimating the American forces in the Wasatch Range, but that the Americans were still clinging to their positions. From Tim Donovan he learned that the Big Berthas in the captured fortifications had completely demolished all the mills in the Pittsburgh area; but he also learned that the Central Empire had employed a new system of airplane transportation for troops, to fly five divisions of Purple soldiers into the Pittsburgh area. The immense transport planes of the Purple Empire had delivered those troops virtually at the doorsteps of the Mount Washington fortifications, and the Americans within the fort were now virtually besieged by a force numbering at least twenty thousand troops, with more coming every day.

At first the Central Empire divisions had kept a respectable distance from the fortifications, fearing more shells from the Big Berthas which had destroyed the steel mills.

But they soon discovered that the Americans had no more ammunition for those Big Berthas, and they promptly moved up their lines, making their headquarters in the valley of the Golden

The mighty Maximilian Dam was a thing of ruin.

Triangle, just across the Monongahela from Mount Washington Heights. They attacked continuously, giving the Americans not a bit of breathing space. Thus far the hand grenades and machine guns had beaten off every attack. But there were casualties among the Americans each time, and the small force was being rapidly depleted, while the Central Empire troops increased in number day by day.

ONE BIT of news that was not so disheartening came from New York by way of Z-7 in the Wasatch Mountains. This concerned the coronation of the Emperor. The concerted rebellions which had occurred on Saturday night had caused Rudolph to postpone the coronation. In many of the cities, the rebellions had been ruthlessly stamped out; but in a number of others the rebels had struck telling blows and had then taken refuge in mountainous sections or in the limitless plains of the West, and were causing much trouble to the Central Empire troops sent to stamp out the disturbances.

Rudolph had sworn that he would see America completely pacified before his coronation date—that he would force America to beg him to become its Emperor. And he had accordingly postponed the coronation ceremony for one month

Jimmy Christopher had waited, eaten by a gnawing anxiety for news of Nan and Sergeant MacTavish. He dreaded the news that they had been executed. It was Z-7 who informed him over the radio that those two were being saved for the coronation ceremony one month hence. Rudolph was bound to have them die at his coronation, and he had returned them to jail to await that date.

142

It was just before crossing the Pennsylvania State Line that the last of the gasoline for the motorized infantry gave out. The cavalry now became the swiftest arm of Sir John Batten's division.

A council of war was held, at which the commanding colonels of the four regiments were present, together with Sir John and Operator 5. Jimmy Christopher had given up hope of bringing this division down to the relief of the besieged Americans on Mount Washington. He was now anxious to work his way through the enemy territory and into the fortifications, to take active charge.

So he suggested that Sir John's division make camp here in the devastated area where they would not be bothered, and settle down for the winter. There were plenty of friendly American farmers in the neighborhood who would bring supplies to the men, and the Canadians could pass the cold months virtually unmolested.

But Operator 5 had reckoned without the reckless courage of these brave men. Though the infantry commanders agreed that it would be folly to push on through the severe weather on foot, Colonel Foster of the cavalry regiment insisted on advancing.

"It's no good, Operator 5," Colonel Foster insisted. "It's no good arguing, I tell you. The Canadian Lancers are not afraid to die. We are going forward."

Sir John Batten suggested mildly: "From here on, Operator 5, I insist upon turning over the command of this division to you. It was our original intention to offer to serve under the American command. Now, if you wish to accept our services, we will gladly follow you. If you refuse, we will advance on our initiative. But retreat—never!"

"But look here, Sir John," Jimmy Christopher protested, "you admit that the infantry will have to remain behind. That means just a single regiment of cavalry marching through enemy territory. Once we cross into Pennsylvania, we will meet the fortified oil district around Bradford. You will have fight after fight on your hands, against fearful odds. You know what little chance cavalry has against artillery. Wouldn't it be wiser for the cavalry to remain here in camp with the infantry—"

"No, no. We wouldn't hear of it!" Sir John exclaimed. "We are advancing, Operator 5, with or without you—but *we are advancing!*"

Jimmy Christopher shrugged. "All right, then, but I doubt if one of you will ever see Canada again. Whatever happens though, I salute you as the bravest of men!"

The next morning the cavalry column resumed its march, leaving behind the infantry, with the almost exhausted supply train.

THE COUNTRY had become quite mountainous, and foraging was very difficult now, but the cavalry pushed on, nevertheless, keeping in contact with the bivouacked infantry by means of a system of runners.

Now they began to see occasional signs of habitation, and soon they came in contact with the enemy. From here on their progress was no longer a secret.

The road wound through the mountains, and enemy snipers were thrown into the ridges on both sides to harry them. They rode through this gauntlet of fire for almost an hour, losing close to fifty men, until the road emerged from the mountains and a rising plateau spread before them.

From here they had a splendid view of the enemy entrenchments, and of the spreading oil fields to the south and the east. It was apparent that the. Purple Empire was doing everything in its power to protect these oil fields from destruction. The road was blocked here by a battery of guns which had been placed on the rising ground on either side of the road. Low breastworks had been erected to protect the battery, and the guns commanded every approach to the town of Bradford.

Sir John Batten raised his hand in signal to halt, and the long column of cavalry came to a stop. Sir John turned to Jimmy Christopher, who was riding at his right, while Colonel Foster rode at the General's left. The General's eyes were flashing with eagerness.

"It looks as if we'll have to charge, Operator 5," he said.

Jimmy Christopher looked skeptical. He had discarded his Central Empire uniform and moustache, as being no longer of any use to him, and he had borrowed a spare uniform from one of the men. He spoke slowly.

"If you look behind the enemy batteries, you'll see that they're concentrating infantry in the road behind. To charge those guns would cost you half your regiment, Sir John. After you get past them, you'll have the infantry to contend with."

"And once we're past this position," Sir John Batten asked, "what then?"

"We'd have clear sailing almost as far as Pittsburgh," Jimmy told him. We could cut through the Allegheny National Forest, and we wouldn't encounter any enemy troops until we reached the Allegheny County Line."

Sir John Batten glanced across at Colonel Foster, then looked squarely at Jimmy Christopher.

"Do you want to turn back, Operator 5?" he asked softly.

Jimmy Christopher glanced up the slope toward the batteries of the enemy. A bugle was sounding behind the Purple batteries. No doubt the wires were humming with appeals for more troops to be sent to Bradford. If they attacked now, there was a slim chance of success—and if they won, they would have the oil fields at their mercy. But Jimmy Christopher would not deliberately ask these men to hurl themselves into the mouths of those cannons.

"That is not for me to say, Sir John," Jimmy Christopher told him. "They're your men, and you know their temper and their metal."

Sir John Batten laughed shortly. "I know them well enough! They're aching for a fight. I doubt if I could hold them back."

"Then—let's charge!" Operator 5 exclaimed.

It was a mad, reckless thing to do. It has been generally admitted that cavalry has outgrown its usefulness as an arm of offense or defense. It has been used in modern warfare for mopping up and for scouting, and during the Purple Invasion several cavalry units had been formed in the West which had done good service. But not since the Charge of the Light Brigade at Balaklava has cavalry been used to attack big guns. Operator 5 knew all this very well, but he also knew that these men would not stop until they had taken those guns—even if only fifty of them reached the emplacement.

Sir John Batten said simply: "Let's shake hands, Operator 5—in case we don't meet again."

Sir John, Jimmy and Colonel Foster shook hands. Then Sir John Batten raised his hand in signal, and the trumpet sounded: *Charge!*

SWORDS FLASHED in the sunlight as the long cavalry swung into motion, moving up the slope. Sir John and Colonel Foster raced to be the first, but Jimmy Christopher kept pace with them. And a long yell of exultation arose from the ranks of the mounted men behind them. Down the line, a Canadian trooper raised an American flag, in tribute to Operator 5. The hoofs of the horses drumming on the road sounded a tattoo of gallantry as the Canadian Lancers rode into action. And as if that had been a signal to the enemy, the long wicked guns at the top of the slope began to thunder and vomit fire and lead.

Shells began to burst in the road, and the thunder of the artillery drowned the shouts of the cavalry. The Battle of Bradford had begun.

This battle will go down in history with legendary acts of heroism, taking its place beside that other famous Charge of the Light Brigade at Balaklava.

Men began to fall on every side, and stumbling horses crushed men's bodies into the hard snow. The road became littered with dead and dying, with wounded men and with horses whose entrails stained the snow. The guns thundered their mighty messages of death and destruction, and the air turned thick with cordite, but the Canadian Lancers charged on.

Now they were within a hundred yards of the emplacements, and the Purple Infantry opened up with rifle fire.

Jimmy Christopher, riding far in the lead with Colonel Foster and General Batten, could almost detect the appearance of a note of frantic desperation in the thunder of those guns. Glancing swiftly behind him, he saw that fully half of the column had been annihilated. But those who remained still rode on with exultant shouts. A horse stumbled at Jimmy's left, but he could spare only a glance. That glance showed him Sir John Batten being flung headlong from his mount.

The riders behind Jimmy swerved to avoid stamping out Sir John's life with the iron-shod hooves of their horses. Now the enemy's guns were doing little damage, for the gunners were unable to lower the sights quickly enough.

But the infantry marksmen were picking off the riders with swift sureness. Colonel Foster was hurled from his horse with a bullet between the eyes. Men were falling in the column behind Jimmy Christopher, but he rode on, heedless of the whining slugs that sped through the air. It was as if he bore a charmed life—as if he were reserved for some greater destiny. With his sword flashing in the air he urged the men forward.

And those men needed no urging. Now they reached a level with the enemy replacements, and Jimmy jumped his horse over the low breastwork, slashing with his sabre at the infantry men who were frantically jamming bayonets onto their rifles.

Now the advantage of cavalry was demonstrated. Once they

were out of the direct fire of those big guns, they wreaked dreadful havoc among the demoralized Purple Infantry. Flashing sabres slashed and thrust at the fear-stricken Purple troopers. Central Empire officers screamed at their men to stand and fight.

But the troopers had witnessed that unbelievable charge of these Canadian madmen up that slope; they had seen them ride into the face of the big guns, had seen them ride through bursting shells, had seen them ride on while a full half of them were slaughtered. Before such courage, such fierceness, the Central Empire Infantry could not stand. Suddenly, almost as one man, they turned to flee in wild panic. And the Canadian cavalrymen followed them closely, cutting them down, giving no quarter.

The Charge of the Canadian Lancers had won. The position was taken!

JIMMY CHRISTOPHER dismounted, shouting swift orders in a stentorian voice. He succeeded in separating fifty of the cavalrymen, and ordered them to dismount, to take charge of the guns. So swiftly had that charge won the field, that the enemy artillery had not had time to spike or destroy the cannon. The guns were still intact, and Jimmy Christopher shouted to the dismounted men: "Get up those guns! Swing them around to command the oil field!"

The men grasped his idea at once, and set to work willingly. Jimmy sped from gun to gun, giving the inexperienced men swift instructions in how to handle them. Soon the light guns had been swung around, and under Jimmy's directions were loaded and fired. Jimmy himself had aimed each of those guns, and as the battery thundered in unison, he saw the destruction that the shells were wreaking.

Twice more the battery fired in unison, and then the work was done. Great geysers of smoke and flame were rising into the sky from the oil fields. The Central Empire would never draw oil from this section again.

After the last round was fired, the men spiked the guns, then mounted at Jimmy's order and followed the main body of cavalry into the town of Bradford.

Under Jimmy Christopher's orders, a number of trucks and automobiles were rounded up, and the civilians were loaded into them, started back on the road toward the winter quarters of the balance of the Canadian Division.

The cavalrymen who had been wounded in the charge and in the subsequent fighting were also placed on the trucks after being given medical attention. General Batten was still alive. He had been shot in the shoulder at the same time that his horse had been hit, and though he protested that he wanted to go on, Jimmy Christopher insisted that he return to the winter quarters.

The Canadian horsemen enthusiastically agreed to follow Jimmy Christopher. They worked fast, and an hour after Bradford had been taken, the last of the civilians and the wounded soldiers had been started on their way north, while Jimmy Christopher rode south at the head of the column. The casualties had been enormous. Of twelve hundred men who had begun that charge, only five hundred now rode after Operator 5. But those five hundred now carried with them a glory and a tradition that would never die. They had taken part in the most spectacular battle of modern times—and they had emerged victorious.

Operator 5 felt a strange thrill of confidence. He had come through the battle unwounded and now he felt that if he could reach Pittsburgh with these five hundred men behind him, nothing would be impossible for them....

CHAPTER 11
THE LAST SHELL

I N THE city of Pittsburgh, the Central Empire troops were solidly massed in the triangle formed by the junction of the Allegheny and Monongahela Rivers. Twenty thousand infantry were spread out across the Monongahela from the Mount Washington Heights. Enemy artillery had been brought into place in many positions on heights which made a perfect target of the fortifications.

They had been shelling those fortifications continuously for eight days, and the constant din and thunder of those great guns drummed a funeral chant of death into the tired ears of the defenders under Frank Ames. The fort itself was demolished. Concrete and steel had not been able to withstand the devastating impact of those huge shells. The breastworks were breached in a dozen places, too, but the machine-gun mounds still resisted.

But now a new danger threatened. For six days the enemy had been dropping caissons into the river, from which men were boring into the cliffs.

Frank Ames had watched these operations through field glasses from one of the machine-gun mounds behind the first line of breastworks. At first he had been puzzled, not understanding the enemy's intention.

As he watched, he suddenly understood. His face grew pale, and he turned to Tim Donovan who was crouching in the machine gun nest beside him.

"I tell you, Tim," he exclaimed, "that's what they're going to do. They're tunneling under the mountain, and they're going to load it with dynamite, then explode it into kingdom come. We've got to stop them."

"Look, Mr. Ames," Tim suggested, "we have one shell left for one of the Big Berthas. Why not try to drop it on the river? It might do enough damage to stop the tunneling operations."

"It won't do," Ames said. "They've got caissons right here below us, and they've got others about a mile up the river. However, we'll try it. Let's go."

They climbed down the spiral staircase into the underground chamber, and made their way back toward the fourth series of breastworks. It was here that the single remaining shell was being kept for use in one of the Big Berthas.

They passed women and children in the subterranean passages, who were sitting about in despair, stunned by the continuous gunfire. In one corner, on a bed which had been brought in here, a husband was leaning solicitously over his dying wife.

AT THAT moment one of the Americans came running through the room, and spied their group. He ran up to them, exclaimed: "Tim Donovan! You're wanted on the radio. Operator 5 talking!"

Tim exclaimed: "Why! He must be close now."

The three of them hurried through the underground rooms, into the radio room. Tim Donovan donned the ear phones. In a moment he was talking to Operator 5.

"Where are you now, Jimmy?" he asked quickly.

Jimmy's voice came to him over the ether. Operator 5 was using the radio he had salvaged from his plane, and which he had brought along.

"I'm at the Freedom Airport, where we met Ames originally. We can't advance any closer without running into the enemy. I've sent out scouts, and they report that the Purple troops are as thick as flies around Pittsburgh. What's your situation there?"

"It's bad, Jimmy. We've got enough food, but the water is running out. I don't have to tell you about the drumfire; you can hear it from where you are. The enemy are tunneling in under the cliff from the river, and they're probably going to dynamite us. We have one shell left, and we're going to use it to try to destroy the caissons—"

"Wait, Tim!" Jimmy Christopher's voice was suddenly taut with excitement. "You have one shell left, you say?"

"That's right, Jimmy. Why?"

"Look here, Tim. You tell Ames to put his best gunners on this job. Load that Big Bertha, and *sight it carefully at the Maximilian Dam!* Do you understand?"

For a moment Tim Donovan was stunned into silence. Then

he breathed: "Boy, oh boy! What an idea! Here we go, Jimmy. Watch us!"

He ripped the ear phones from his ears, swung excitedly to Ames, and told him what Jimmy had suggested.

Ames' face lighted up, and he snapped his fingers. "Why the devil didn't we think of that ourselves!"

He raced through the adjoining subterranean chambers, until he came to the emplacement where the Big Bertha was located. Swiftly he communicated the plan to the men in charge of the gun.

"I'm going to sight this myself," he told them. *"And there must be no such thing as a miss!"*

Quickly the word spread through the fortifications of what they intended to do. Men, women and children gathered around the Big Bertha, in massed expectancy. Others flocked to the peepholes of the machine-gun mounds, to get a view of the dam.

Ames took charge of sighting the gun, and checked everything to the last detail.

At last he stood back satisfied, sang out crisply: "Fire!"

The Big Bertha shuddered with the recoil of the discharge, and they all waited with breathless expectancy while the huge shell sped through the air.

SUDDENLY THEY heard the thunderous detonation as the shell of the Big Bertha struck its target. And then, as if in echo of that explosion, there came to their ears a deep-throated, mighty rumbling as of a thousand giants growling in wrath. That rumbling noise grew louder and louder until it swirled into a shuddering roar.

"It struck! It struck!" Ames shouted almost hysterically.

Heedless of danger, they all raced up the ramp into the open. The enemy artillery had ceased firing and they looked to the northwest to see what their shell had done. It had done everything that was expected of it.

The mighty Maximilian Dam was only a thing of ruin.

The great intake towers at either side still stood, but the concrete dam across the Ohio River had virtually disappeared.

The scene down there across the river was one of panic and terror. Purple troopers fled pell-mell, trampling upon each other, thrusting each other out of their way, in the wild effort to escape that mighty avenging torrent which swept down upon them.

But human legs could never be so fast as a raging river unleashed from its penning dam. The swirling waters overtook the fleeing soldiers, swept over them, carrying them off downstream. All that valley between the Allegheny and the Monongahela became like a great lake in which twenty thousand Purple troopers were swept to destruction.

Frank Ames raised a shaking hand to his eyes.

Diane Elliot put a hand on his arm. "It was well done, Mr. Ames," she said.

Tim Donovan was almost shivering with the intensity of his feeling. "We've put it over!" he exclaimed.

The lad left the group, hurried down into the subterranean chambers to the radio room to communicate the effect of the explosion to Jimmy Christopher.

"Jimmy!" he exclaimed. "The Purple Army is wiped out. Your

idea did it. The flood carried them away. You can march in now, with your cavalry!"

Operator 5's voice came back to Tim Donovan, pitched in a sober tone. "That's great, Jimmy. I'm sorry for those men who perished, but it was the only thing. When the water subsides, I'll ride in with my men."

"Gosh, Jimmy, it means victory. Now we can hold this place—"

"No, Tim, we won't be able to hold this place. There's work for us elsewhere."

"What do you mean?" Tim Donovan detected the note of urgency in Jimmy Christopher's voice.

"I've been on the radio myself," Jimmy told him. "I've just gotten news. Rudolph has landed a huge consignment of a secret type of ordnance, which was manufactured in the Skoda factories in Europe. That ordnance is now on its way to the Rockies. We've got to head it off!"

The boy's shoulders sagged. "Gosh, Jimmy, how'll we head it off—right in the heart of the enemy territory?"

"We'll manage somehow, kid," Jimmy Christopher told him grimly. "After the things that the Americans and the Canadians have done this far, nothing at all is impossible!"

POPULAR HERO PULPS AVAILABLE NOW:

CAPTAIN COMBAT
- ❑ #1: The Sky Beast of Berlin — $13.95
- ❑ #2: Red Wings For the Blood Battalion — $13.95

CAPTAIN ZERO
- ❑ #1: City of Deadly Sleep — $13.95
- ❑ #2: The Mark of Zero! — $13.95
- ❑ #3: The Golden Murder Syndicate — $13.95

OPERATOR 5
- ❑ #1: The Masked Invasion — $13.95
- ❑ #2: The Invisible Empire — $13.95
- ❑ #3: The Yellow Scourge — $13.95
- ❑ #4: The Melting Death — $13.95
- ❑ #5: Cavern of the Damned — $13.95
- ❑ #6: Master of Broken Men — $13.95
- ❑ #7: Invasion of the Dark Legions — $13.95
- ❑ #8: The Green Death Mists — $13.95
- ❑ #9: Legions of Starvation — $13.95
- ❑ #10: The Red Invader — $13.95
- ❑ #11: The League of War-Monsters — $13.95
- ❑ #12: The Army of the Dead — $13.95
- ❑ #13: March of the Flame Marauders — $13.95
- ❑ #14: Blood Reign of the Dictator — $13.95
- ❑ #15: Invasion of the Yellow Warlords — $13.95
- ❑ #16: Legions of the Death Master — $13.95
- ❑ #17: Hosts of the Flaming Death — $13.95
- ❑ #18: Invasion of the Crimson Death Cult — $13.95
- ❑ #19: Attack of the Blizzard Men — $13.95
- ❑ #20: Scourge of the Invisible Death — $13.95
- ❑ #21: Raiders of the Red Death — $13.95
- ❑ #22: War-Dogs of the Green Destroyer — $13.95
- ❑ #23: Rockets From Hell — $13.95
- ❑ #24: War-Masters from the Orient — $13.95
- ❑ #25: Crime's Reign of Terror — $13.95
- ❑ #26: Death's Ragged Army — $13.95
- ❑ #27: Patriots' Death Battalion — $13.95
- ❑ #28: The Bloody Forty-five Days — $13.95
- ❑ #29: America's Plague Battalions — $13.95
- ❑ #30: Liberty's Suicide Legions — $13.95
- ❑ *NEW:* #31: Siege of the Thousand Patriots — $13.95

DUSTY AYRES AND HIS BATTLE BIRDS
- ❑ #1: Black Lightning! — $13.95
- ❑ #2: Crimson Doom — $13.95
- ❑ #3: The Purple Tornado — $13.95
- ❑ #4: The Screaming Eye — $13.95
- ❑ #5: The Green Thunderbolt — $13.95
- ❑ #6: The Red Destroyer — $13.95
- ❑ #7: The White Death — $13.95
- ❑ #8: The Black Avenger — $13.95
- ❑ #9: The Silver Typhoon — $13.95
- ❑ #10: The Troposphere F-S — $13.95
- ❑ #11: The Blue Cyclone — $13.95
- ❑ #12: The Tesla Raiders — $13.95

MAVERICKS
- ❑ #1: Five Against the Law — $12.95
- ❑ #2: Mesquite Manhunters — $12.95
- ❑ #3: Bait for the Lobo Pack — $12.95
- ❑ #4: Doc Grimson's Outlaw Posse — $12.95
- ❑ #5: Charlie Parr's Gunsmoke Cure — $12.95

THE MYSTERIOUS WU FANG
- ❑ #1: The Case of the Six Coffins — $12.95
- ❑ #2: The Case of the Scarlet Feather — $12.95
- ❑ #3: The Case of the Yellow Mask — $12.95
- ❑ #4: The Case of the Suicide Tomb — $12.95
- ❑ #5: The Case of the Green Death — $12.95
- ❑ #6: The Case of the Black Lotus — $12.95
- ❑ #7: The Case of the Hidden Scourge — $12.95

THE SECRET 6
- ❑ #1: The Red Shadow — $13.95
- ❑ #2: House of Walking Corpses — $13.95
- ❑ #3: The Monster Murders — $13.95
- ❑ #4: The Golden Alligator — $13.95